INDEPENDENT MONTHLY LITERARY MAGAZINE

Adelaide

REVISTA LITERÁRIA INDEPENDENTE MENSAL

ADELAIDE

Independent Monthly Literary Magazine
Revista Literária Independente Mensal
Year III, Number 13, May 2018
Ano III, Número 13, maio de 2018

ISBN-13: 978-1-949180-03-9
ISBN-10: 1-949180-03-4

Adelaide Literary Magazine is an independent international monthly publication, based in New York and Lisbon. Founded by Stevan V. Nikolic and Adelaide Franco Nikolic in 2015, the magazine's aim is to publish quality poetry, fiction, nonfiction, artwork, and photography, as well as interviews, articles, and book reviews, written in English and Portuguese. We seek to publish outstanding literary fiction, nonfiction, and poetry, and to promote the writers we publish, helping both new, emerging, and established authors reach a wider literary audience.

A Revista Literária Adelaide é uma publicação mensal internacional e independente, localizada em Nova Iorque e Lisboa. Fundada por Stevan V. Nikolic e Adelaide Franco Nikolic em 2015, o objectivo da revista é publicar poesia, ficção, não-ficção, arte e fotografia de qualidade assim como entrevistas, artigos e críticas literárias, escritas em inglês e português. Pretendemos publicar ficção, não-ficção e poesia excepcionais assim como promover os escritores que publicamos, ajudando os autores novos e emergentes a atingir uma audiência literária mais vasta.

(http://adelaidemagazine.org)

Published by: Adelaide Books, New York
244 Fifth Avenue, Suite D27
New York NY, 10001
e-mail: info@adelaidemagazine.org
phone: (917) 727 8907
http://adelaidebooks.org

FOUNDERS / FUNDADORES
Stevan V. Nikolic & Adelaide Franco Nikolic

EDITOR IN CHIEF / EDITOR-CHEFE
Stevan V. Nikolic
editor@adelaidemagazine.org

ASSOCIATE EDITOR
Raymond Fenech

MANAGING DIRECTOR / DIRECTORA EXECUTIVA
Adelaide Franco Nikolic

GRAPHIC & WEB DESIGN
Adelaide Books DBA, New York

CONTRIBUTING AUTHORS IN THIS ISSUE

Dimitra Tsourou,
Malika McCoy,
Deanna M. Lehman,
Betty J. Sayles,
Vanya Suchan,
Cassie Follman,
Allen Long,
Kevin Gillam,
James K. Zimmerman,
Ross Jackson,
Talon Florig,
Patrick Erickson,
Daniel Ruefman,
Danielle Hanson,
John Sweet,
Souzi Gharib,
Olga Kawecka,
William Pruitt,
Stephanie Daich,
Rikki Santer,
Melanie Ann,
John Richmond,
Michele Sprague Sulkowski,
Jesse Kemmerer,
Tom Lakin,
Raymond Tatten,
David Massey,
Amada Matei,
Barbara Bottner,
Ewa Hanna Mazierska,
Hina Ahmed,
Zia Marshall,
Annina Lavee,
Sharon Frame Gay,
Jose Manuel Sánchez,
Cassidy Manley,
Edward Lee,
Roger Singer,

CONTENTS / CONTEÚDOS

Editor's Notes
Stevan V. Nikolic

THOUGHTS & QUOTES

"Strangely enough, he didn't feel any guilt for separating himself from his past. Five years ago, he clearly heard in his dream a message brought to him by Archangel Michael from the God Almighty, telling him he should get up and leave everything behind; that his place was not there; that it was time to go in search for his true self and for his true destiny. Now, five years after, he was sitting in the Bowery chapel, a broken and homeless man, still trying to find that which he was looking for. But he didn't regret anything he had done in those five years. In his mind, it wasn't his doing. He sincerely believed that he surrendered his own will to the will of God and that everything that happened to him, good or bad, had to happen for some reason. It was God's doing. It was his destiny. He just had to figure out why." — **Stevan V. Nikolic,** *Truth According to Michael*

"How far we can go with our liberty of conscience, without offending God, and disturbing the natural order of things…" — **Stevan V. Nikolic,** *Truth According to Michael*

"Sometimes, he thought of himself as an elephant walking through the china store, breaking everything in his path and still expecting people not to be angry with the damage he made, but rather to admire his strength and his endurance."
— **Stevan V. Nikolic,** *Truth According to Michael*

"I was going after a woman believing that the key is in being with her. But the key is in writing about her. The key is in words and words are in me. Longing for her is just an impulse for words to come out. And the whole purpose is for words to come out. Words are important. Words about love. About life." — **Stevan V. Nikolic,** *Truth According to Michael*

"I don't know why I am doing this. Everybody is saying bad things about you. Wherever you go, whatever you do, there is a noise after you… In spite of everything, I respect your courage to go after your ideals, no matter what. Men like you make this world move. I know that the road you go is covered with thorns. But I also know that it must be a road to the stars."
— **Stevan V. Nikolic,** *Truth According to Michael*

"The truth of the matter was that Michael was arrogant and selfish. He never had a respect for anything or anybody. Whatever he was doing in his life, he was never happy. There was always something that he missed, that would make him leave everything and disappear and he didn't know why." — **Stevan V. Nikolic,** *Truth According to Michael*

"You know, Michael," Pastor Charles would often tell him, "some men get high on drugs and make a mess while they are high; others get drunk and behave like animals while under the influence of alcohol; and you Michael, you fall in love and lose any sense of reality. It is the same like getting high. You are an addict too. You are addicted to women. But not in the perverted pornographic or sexual way. Sex is just a part of it. Your addiction is more about love. You are addicted to falling in love. And the only remedy for your addiction is the ultimate love; love of God and love for God. Turn to God Michael. He loves you. Show your love for him and you will be healed." — **Stevan V. Nikolic,** *Truth According to Michael*

THE TROUBLE WITH BOREDOM

by Melanie A. Doan

Marty looks at me over the rims of his aviators, which are held together by a piece of Scotch tape in the middle. "So, how exactly do you expect us to pull this little stunt off, Joe?" he asks.

I look at my twin with a smirk on my lips, and I know he sees the twinkle in my eye. I can feel it. Just like I always do when I come up with a great plan. "Exactly as we'd planned, bro. Clean sweep."

Marty sighs. "We're talking about grand theft auto here, not Good Housekeeping."

"Do you want to get your car back or not?" I ask as I look at the sky. Grey clouds are sweeping in from the southwest, and with the increase in humidity, I'd bet my left nut that there will be tornado warnings this evening. My brother and I are sitting on the front porch of our mother's house, and even though we aren't moving, sweat is dripping off our foreheads and into our water-downed Bud Lights. I recall the first time I saw Pops drink it. He used to call it piss water.

Good ol' Pops. He'd be proud of the plan I've devised.

See, Marty and I grew up in this little hick town in southern Alabama where crime is swept under the rug because there is only one sheriff in a town of just under five hundred people. The closest prison is two hours away, so the worst punishment most criminals get is a slap on the wrist and one night in lock-up, depending on the severity of the crime. The most anyone has ever stayed in lock-up was eight nights. Everyone knows the story of Old Lady Jane. She caught her husband cheating on her with her younger sister – who was way prettier, and everyone knew it - so she poisoned her husband with arsenic in his daily coffee. The poor ol' bastard never saw his death comin'. Since this was the first time anyone had committed murder in our town, Jane got eight days in lock-up then moved up north to live with her daughter in Boston.

I don't know why Marty is so worried about what we're going to do. I mean, it was his car that was stolen, and it's his car that we're stealing back. The law will be on our side.

"Why can't we just go and ask Tommy for the car back? It'd make things so much easier. It's too darn hot to go runnin' around and makin' sure there's no one on my tail ready to throw me into the cell."

I take a swig of booze from the bottle, and peel off the sticker which is melting away from the glass. This side of Marty annoys me. I'm ready to just leave him out of this whole situation and get the car back myself. He's too much of a goody-two-shoes for me anyway. We may be identical twins, but when it comes to our personalities, Marty's got a pair of white angel wings stickin' outta his damn back. And me? My halo's bein' held up by my pointy red horns.

"Marty, you gotta take some risks in your life. No risk, no reward. Tommy took a risk in stealing your car. His reward? He gets to drive around in a nice, air conditioned Ford Mustang until we go and take it back from him."

Marty pulls his white Hanes t-shirt off his torso and tosses it over the banister into the yard. "Joe, you can't make a livin' bein' a thief. It just ain't worth it. Eventually Sheriff Thompson is goin' to get tired of seein' you and send you to the state penitentiary so he won't have to deal with you no mo'. And what will Mama do if either one of us is taken away? She'll die of heartbreak."

Damn that Marty! He always has to rain on my parade by bringin' our innocent Mama into the mix. Then again, what Mama don't know won't hurt her...

Marty uses the cue of the settin' sun to go inside and make sure Mama takes her medication. I'm in the same wooden rockin' chair I've been in all damn day. From sun up til sun down, this is where I stay. It's where I do my best thinkin' before I run off into the dead of night to do what I do best: steal from those who have been stolen from. It's kind of a weird gig. I don't get paid for it, and I don't want to get paid. It's just the right thing to do, ya know what I'm sayin'? And now that my own brother has fell victim to these crimes, I've gots to work extra hard to make sure justice is given to the sorry son of a bitch who decided to mess with him.

Marty sometimes joins me on my excursions around town, but usually he stays with Mama. She tends to sleep walk and has been known to escape the house in her white nightie that is way too big for her and falls farther down her front side than it needs to. I've tried giving her a new one every year at Christmas for the past seven years, and each year she says, "What the hell do I need this for? The one I have on is perfectly fine!"

Marty has a big mouth – a trait he picked up from Mama. And that is why I like to do my own work on my own terms. I promised him I'll get his car back from Tommy, and lucky for me Tommy works nights over at The Salty Pig, the twenty-four hour BBQ pit and dive bar.

"Alright Marty. I'm headin' out," I say as I pull my John Deere ball cap over my balding head. "Mama had her glass of milk with her medicine, right?"

"Yes, Boss, she did. You act like I don't know what to do with her," Marty said, his voice clouded with disdain.

I ignore the dramatics; that's another thing Marty is good for. He is such a passive aggressive brat when he doesn't get his way. "I'll be home after midnight, like usual."

"You sure you don't want me to go with you, Joe? I mean, you don't have to steal the car back. We know Tommy; all we'll have to do is ask him," he explains as he our dad's old bottle of JD from the back of the medicine cabinet and pours himself a shot.

"That's not the point of my operation, little brother," I say as I grab the bottle of whiskey from him and take a sip straight from the bottle. "And besides, this isn't a typical Robin Hood excursion." A few drops of liquid jump out from the bottle as I set it on the counter.

Marty turned his head towards me after throwing back his shot. "It's not?"

"No. This time, the thief messed with my family." I enjoy another swig of liquor. "So I'm going to mess with his."

"No!" Marty yells as I open the screen door and step onto the front porch. "Just go get my car back, Joe. Please? I beg you! Don't make this a bigger deal than it already is."

I look at my chest when I realize Marty's fists are grasping onto my shirt collar. His eyes are wide with panic at the thought of anything violent taking place in our peaceful little town. I am still deciding whether I'm going to listen to him or not when he says,

"I'll tell Mama."

I shove him against the door frame. "The hell you will! We made a pact, Marty James. A blood pact which clearly states that Mama is to never know about my hobby as a vigilante."

"Then I go with you."

A deep groan escaped my chest and I hung my head, still keeping a grip on Marty's shoulders. I don't want to risk our Mama's safety by having us both out of the house; but on the same token, I can't risk Mama's sanity if she knew her firstborn son wasn't the blessed child she always makes me out to be. My heart pounds against my rib cage as guilt flows through my veins. "You sad, son of a bitch."

"Alright!" Marty yells with a bit too much enthusiasm.

"Shh! Don't wake Mama!"

"Oh! Right," he whispers. "Let me go grab my shoes, then we'll be good to go." His face is lit up like a five year old's on Christmas mornin'. Jesus Christ.

About an hour later, I finally pull into a parking spot at the rear of The Salty Pig. It's one of a handful of restaurants in town, and it's the best one. Pops used to own the place back in its prime, and the recipes used by the chefs today are from his own imagination. It's a shame to see the outside of the place looking like it's gone to shit, but it has. When Tommy's mother bought the place from Pops when he was sick, her focus was solely on bringing in the dough. And the best BBQ in the south is cooked up day and night – for the tourists as well as for the town drunks.

The place was built inside two mobile homes that were settled right next to each other; the one on the left – with its cracked aluminum siding – is the giant kitchen where the meat's cut and smoked. It's where the magic happens, as Pops used to say. The buildin' on the right is the seating area for the guests and it also hous- es the bar at the far end of the trailer. About thirty people can enjoy some food and booze at any given time, which is why it's kept open all day and all night. Let's just say Wendy is going to enjoy her retirement when she finally leaves this place.

"Alright Joe, what do we do first?" Marty asks in a whisper as we wait for the hostess to seat us.

I put my hand up to shush him. "Hold on a mi- nute, Little Brother. I'm scopin' the place out."

Marty smiles, as if he just had a lightbulb mo- ment – something he doesn't have very often. "Ah! You're doing recon first. That makes sense!"

"Howdy, boys! What brings you over to these parts?"

Marty and I turn around and see Wendy Mac- Bride walking towards us, her arms open and a big smile on her face. "I haven't ya'll in years! How is your Mama doing?" she asks as she gives us each a hug.

"Mama is Mama. You know how she is," I say.

"Please tell her I say hello. I really should stop over and see her some time!"

"She would really like that, Ma'am," Marty says. I have to stifle a laugh because his cheeks are all pink; he's had a crush on Mrs. MacBride since we were teenagers.

Wendy extends her elbows to link arms with us as she takes us to a pair of open seats at the bar. Even though it has been a while since we've seen her, I gotta admit that she still looks good for her age. She hasn't had any cosmetic work done, but she wears a lot of make-up, and it's obvious she uses an anti-wrinkle cream. But that smile of hers is infectious. Too bad Tommy didn't inherit any of her looks.

"So, what can I get you boys?"

"I'll take a barbecue chicken pizza and a Bud Light please, Ma'am."

"Marty, please, call me Wendy! You're an adult too now; there's no need for the formalities," she said as she patted his arm. "And what can I get for you, sweetie?"

"Just an ice water for now. I'm drivin'."

Wendy lets out a laugh so obnoxious, I can feel the eyes of other customers on our backs. I shift on the barstool and keep my head turned from them. I don't need more people than nec- essary paying attention to me.

"An ice water!? Oh, Joseph. You silly, silly boy. Tell me what you really want." Wendy's hands are on top of mine. She wants the truth? Well, then that's what I'm gonna give her.

I suck in a deep breath of air, and let it out slow before I respond. I want to keep this woman on her toes. "Where is Thomas." It's not a ques- tion; more of a demand.

Wendy's eyes grow to the size of fifty-cent pieces. That means she's scared. Good. "Now Joseph, you know Tommy doesn't want to see you no more. Not after what happened when you stole his woman away."

My eyes roll so far to the back of my head I saw darkness for a moment. "Wendy, we all know that Sarah was leaving Tommy's dumb ass be- cause of his drinkin'. She'd wanted me anyway. From the beginning." I pause to let her think about the facts for a moment. "Tommy stole

Marty's car earlier this mornin', when we were still asleep. I'm here to get it back. Where is he?"

Wendy let out a defeated sigh. "He's over in the other buildin' cuttin' up meats."

I nod my head politely as I get up from my seat. "Thank you. We really appreciate this."

"Do you need me to go with ya, Joe?" Marty asks as Wendy cracks open a bottle of Bud Light for him.

"No." I look at our old friend's mother. "Make sure he stays right there," I say as I point to my brother."

"I'll do my best." The enthusiasm was gone from her voice.

It may have been close to midnight, but that did nothing to save me from turning into a sweaty pig as I crossed the patio that connected the restaurant to the kitchen. Before I stepped into the Roaster (that's what all the chefs called it, because the temperature in there was probably close to one hundred damn degrees), I took my cap off and rubbed the excess moisture from my head. I let out a breath I didn't realize I was holding, and charged through the door to make sure I got Tommy's attention right quick.

"Hey now, you can't be in here!" Ron, the kitchen manager, stormed up to me and tried to push me back out the door. I grabbed his wrists and held him in place.

"Where is Tommy?" I asked as my eyes bore into his.

The poor idiot realized who I was and stammered through his rebuttal. "He-he's-he's, n-n-not here right. Now."

A belly laugh followed suit. "Oh, come on now, Ronnie. I'm a big boy! I can handle Mighty Joe all by myself." Tommie's southern drawl was heavier than everyone else's. Even his laughing carried an accent with it. He took of his plastic gloves as he approached us. "How ya doin', Old Timer?" He gave me a strong pat on the back.

I let go of Ron and turned my attention to Tommy. "Whaddaya doin' with my baby brother's car, ya dirtbag?" I hadn't intended to spit in his face as I spoke, but I was so damn mad I figured it was a nice special effect.

"I don' know what yer talkin' about. I ain't come around to your place since before Sarah and me split."

I don't like to be violent. It's just when I have to deal with little pricks like Tommy – who know they've something wrong, yet try to lie about it anyway – that my blood just boils. And it had nothin' to do with us being in the Roaster, either. "Let's be smart about this, shall we, Tommy? You tell me the truth, and I won't hurt ya. Got it?"

"Honest to God, Joey. I ain't touched yer brother's piece of shit Ford!"

At that moment, Ron came running in through the door, pointing to the parking lot. Red and blue lights were flashing. "Tom, the cops are here. They want to talk to ya."

"Aw shit. What did Mother do now?" Tommy said as he pushed me away from him and ran outside.

"Wendy?" I asked out loud. Why would the cops be here for her? She's the sweetest woman in the world. But not sweeter than Mama, of course.

When I walked into the humid night, I saw Marty standing next to Officer Tompkins, who was in the process of cuffing him. "What the hell, Marty!? I was gone not even ten minutes and you bring the cops here?"

Tears flooded my brother's cheeks. "I'm sorry, Joe. I had to do somethin'! You were takin' too long with Tommy and I just wanted to get my damn car back."

Officer Wade helped Marty protect his head as he got him into the backseat of the cruiser and slammed the door. "A patron over in the restaurant saw your brother hotwiring the car. They thought it was suspicious so they called us."

"Yea but, it's his car! Tommy stole it yesterday mornin' and we was here tryin' to get it back. C'mon, Wade. You know Marty's a good guy! He wouldn't hurt a fly."

The cop shrugged. "Show's how little you know about your brother."

What? Okay, now I'm confused. "What do you mean?"

"He's admitted to being the town's Robin Hood guy we've been tracking down the last six months. While his intentions were noble, stealin' is stealin'. So he's gonna do some time in lock-up."

I had to keep myself from laughin'. That son of a bitch! For once in my life, he actually listened to me! No risk, no reward. Well, he took a risk, and this isn't the reward that most people would be proud of. But let's be honest: in a town like this, you're a celebrity if you spend even one night in lock-up. It'll also give me a break from all the vigilante shit.

And little does Marty know that this stunt he pulled will put me back on the pedestal of being Mama's favorite son. And that's all the reward that I'll ever need.

About the Author:

Melanie A. Doan is an adjunct faculty member at South University in Cleveland, Ohio where she teaches English composition. Melanie achieved her MA from Southern New Hampshire University in May 2015, and earned BFA from Bowling Green State University in December 2011. Her work has appeared in Prairie Margins, where it won the Howard McCord Poetry Award. Mrs. Doan lives in the Cleveland area with her husband and their two cats, Pique and Ember.

THAT SWEET YOUNG "THANG"

by John Richmond

They didn't go looking for anything, no, they just wanted to listen to some good music, but the moment she walked in the door- everything changed.

Their decision to go was one of those last minute things, borne out of the need to do something- besides nothing and stay in the condo- but at the same time their minds kept coming up blank when they tried to think of what it was they could do.

The two of them- Steve and David- paced the rooms, throwing possibilities back and forth until they landed on something that was of interest to both of them- music. And, what cemented the decision was their remembering that some good friends were opening at a club, a little further out on West End.

So, with that settled, they made their way to the strip mall, parked, went in, sat down and ordered a couple of Budweisers.

They drank and listened through the first set, decided that they'd leave after the second- but that was until they saw her walk through the door.

She was young- but still old enough- smartly dressed in a brown leather coat, designer jeans and heels, with a great body and shoulder-length red hair. Alongside of her was what could easily be described as an- at least- octogenarian, managing along with a walker and an oxygen tank.

At first, Steve didn't think of them as being together. No, it wasn't until she stopped to help him along- while putting her hand on top of his- that it dawned on him.

"Hmm," he uttered soft and low and looked over at David. "What do you think?"

"About her?" David replied.

Steve laughed, ever so slightly. "No, not about her- we know about her- she's a sweet young thang," he drawled in a suggestive way. "I'm asking, what about that?" he continued, gesturing toward the two of them with a slight move of his head.

David watched her help the old man along with - he noticed clearly- considerable care and empathy.

"Ah, man," David finally managed in an uncertain tone, "maybe it's her grandfather. Or once upon a time he was a big shit in Nashville, and we either don't know who he is or because he's so old that we just don't recognize him."

"Right- maybe," Steve replied with a definite touch of skepticism.

She stood there, scouting for a table and then- while making more than passing eye-contact with Steve- she decided on one on the far side of the room.

Yet, instead of taking the most direct- and obviously shortest- path to it, she led, guided, if you will, her partner on a way that would take them right past Steve and David's table.

Steve watched her as she navigated her partner ahead of her through a near-like maze of tables and chair legs.

"I guess it's easier to push him ahead of her than drag him from behind," Steve thought to himself.

It wasn't until the old man passed him and she was right next to his chair, did she make serious and prolonged eye contact with Steve before moving on.

After she passed, he took serious note of how well she fit into her skin-tight jeans.

"Very nice," he said in an approving tone and a touch of an appreciative sigh.

Once they were at their table and just before she was completely seated- but after she had helped her partner negotiate the move from the walker to the chair- at that last moment, she looked up and over at Steve and shot him an ever-so-secret smile.

Steve nodded slowly, then turned some portion- but not all- of his attention to what was going on on-stage.

It was after they had finished their second round of drinks, and the waitress was asking if they wanted a third, that Steve decided to up the ante.

"Sure, we'll both have another, and," he paused to look over at the redhead across the room and then back at the waitress, "why don't you give them over there," he motioned with his head, "whatever they're drinking."

"Will do," the waitress said, with a knowing inflection in her tone, after glancing over at the woman and back at Steve.

Steve watched the waitress walk over to the other table to inform them of Steve's intent. Both of them, she with a nod of her head and her partner with a slightly raised, trembling hand in acknowledgement, sent their respective "thank-yous."

Now, Steve shifted his focus to the woman's partner. He was old, much older than he looked at first glance when they walked in the door.

"The guy's got to be in- at least- his late eighties- if not nineties," Steve apprised himself.

He continued to observe the man breathe in a labored manner, taking sips of his drink- it seemed- whenever he was up for it. Occasionally, he reached over and touched the walker and the oxygen tank, almost in a reassuring and comforting way.

Yet, although he looked as if he was taking in the music- and the scene- every now and then, the man would glance away and stare off into the distance with a far-away look in his eyes.

"Boy," Steve continued to himself, "talk about the walking dead."

Steve now turned his attention back on her; how she talked, touched, helped- and even laughed with- the old man. And, as much as they were obviously mismatched, Steve perceived something warm and personal occurring between them.

Oh, there were no obvious and demonstrative acts of intimacy, no kiss on the cheek, no stroking of hair, no gentle touch of the face- but, from what Steve saw, he could easily imagine.

As the night of music progressed, the initial reason for being the club continued to recede into the background. It pretty much accelerated away when Steve decided to reposition his chair, ever so slightly, so that all he had to do was shift his eyes- instead of turning his head- in order to see the band or look at her.

He especially watched each time the waitress served them two more drinks; both the woman and the old man- after being prompted by the woman- raised their glasses in thanks.

Steve and David gestured in kind, after which Steve wondered about how to get to the next step- finding out who she is.

Suddenly, the man began to struggle in his seat. At first, Steve thought that the man was experiencing the beginning of some sort of medical emergency.

Quickly- yet discreetly- he reached over and tapped David on his upper arm. Once he got his attention, he gave him the head-nod in the direction of the other table.

They were both about to get up and go over to help, when they saw the woman stand up and help the man into a standing position behind his walker. Next, she pointed in the direction of the restrooms, said something to him, gently squeezed his forearm, then watched him make his way across the club and around the corner to the men's room.

Once he was out of sight, she sat back down for a moment before she glanced up at Steve and smiled.

Steve kept his eyes on her as she stood, again, and pull at the cuffs of her leather coat, before heading toward their table. She walked purposefully, confidently- even invitingly- exuding a sense that she had more than enough time to do what she intended to do. The three of them greeted each other with smiles after which she began.

"You know, I came over to thank you guys for buying us drinks," she offered as an opening gambit.

David nodded, acceptingly, knowing that her "thank-you" was almost exclusively directed at Steve.

"Our pleasure," David replied.

"Definitely, definitely," Steve concurred, "no problem."

There was an infinitely short pause, but it was enough time to give the three of them enough time to size each other up.

It was Steve who continued.

"Sure, I mean, in today's day and age, I think that it's outstanding that you would take your grandfather out for an evening of music."

The woman looked from Steve to David and back again at Steve, with a smile.

"That's very nice of you to say that, but, he's not my grandfather," she said with a slightly- and almost imperceptibly- larger, more knowing smile.

"Oh," Steve said, now straightening up in his chair as if he had heard the incredible.

"All right," he continued in a sort of self-correcting tone, "your father. I think it's great that you took your father out."

This time, she flashed a sheepish smile at Steve.

"Well," she sighed, "he's not my father."

Steve tilted his head in feigned, confused uncertainty, looked over at David before looking back at the woman.

"H-m-m," Steve uttered thoughtfully, "if he's not your grandfather and if he's not your father, then-" -he paused to take in the moment and allow the obvious to dangle amongst the three of them, before he finished his sentence-

"- who is he?"

With that said, Steve picked up his bottle of beer, took a sip, leaned back and made himself comfortable in his chair.

The woman took a deep breath, puckered her lips, then released a slow and controlled sigh, before she said as simply as possible, "He's my date."

"Ah!" Steve exclaimed as he brought his bottle back down on the table and brought himself up to a forward sitting position.

"Well, that explains everything," he said, as he reached into his pocket, took out his wallet and removed a business card.

"Here," he said offering the card to the woman, "in case your date doesn't make it back from the bathroom, call me and we'll go out to dinner."

She took the card, read it and asked, "Is it Steven or is it Steve?"

Steve looked from the woman to David and back, again. "Steve would be good."

"Okay, Steve" she affirmed, then quickly glanced back toward her table before opening her purse.

"I've got just the place for this-" she began while she put his card in her wallet, "-and, I will take you up on that dinner invitation, but in the meantime- here."

With a smooth and fluid motion, she took her own business card out of her purse and handed it to him.

"That's me and that's where I work. I take lunch starting at twelve-thirty. Can you be there, tomorrow?"

Steve looked at the card, read it, looked up at her and said, "Pamela, twelve-thirty it is," and proceeded to put the card in his coat pocket.

Again, she looked back at her table- and beyond toward the bathroom.

"I'd better get back," she told them.

David nodded while Steve simply said, "Sure, sure thing."

She turned, stopped, turned back and asked, "You will be there- won't you?"

Steve smiled and said, "Absolutely. I'll probably even be there a few minutes early."

"See you tomorrow," she replied, turned, walked back to her table, sat down- and waited.

About the Author:

John Richmond has "wandered" parts of North America for a good portion of his life. These "wanderings" have taken him from a city on the Great Lakes to a small fishing village (population 200), before heading to Tennessee, Georgia, North Carolina and then on to a bigger city on the Great Lakes- Chicago- then, eventually, New York City. Since then, John Richmond has made his way to a small upstate New York town and has sequestered himself in his office where he divides his time between writing and discussing the state of the world with his coonhound buddy- Roma. Recently, he has appeared in Ygdrasil (Canada) (2), Oddball Magazine, Lipstick Party Magazine, Hackwriters (U.K.), Quail Bell Magazine, StepAway Magazine (U.K.), The Potomac (2), Peacock Journal, Embodied Effigies (2), Streetcake Magazine (U.K.), Former People Journal (2), The Other Story, Nazar-Look (Romania) (2), Lavender Wolves, Indiana Voice Journal, Fuck Fiction, The Greensilk Journal, The Corner Club Press, Danse Macabre du Jour, The Tower Journal, Stone Path Review, Meat for Tea: The Valley Review, Rogue Particles Magazine, From the Depths, Flash Frontier (N. Z.), The Birmingham Arts Journal, riverbabble (2), The Writing Disorder, Lalitamba, Poetic Diversity, Marco Polo Arts Magazine, ken*again (2), Black & White, SNReview, Voices de Luna, The Round, Syndic Literary Journal, Slow Trains, Forge Journal, and is forthcoming in Birmingham Arts Journal, Voices de la Luna, and Pudding Magazine.

A GIANT

by William Pruitt

A boy looked at himself in the mirror. He made a face to scare himself.

He went out into the woods. He shouted a made-up word. He ran back to his house, fear overwhelming him.

In church, the pastor warned the Devil was everywhere. The pews were hard and shiny. The songbooks in their bins were closed and distant. The boy thought of Bela Lugosi. He imagined a face, a stare, that held him. He was in that story and was not able to see the story, sitting on the pew, the preacher's words like flies, annoying but not as powerful as the image of the stare. He could not think of what the people sitting around him imagined. Their minds felt blunt, impregnable, dead. He was sitting in a graveyard.

The boy grew up and freed himself. He looked around and noticed everybody was behind the eight ball until they stepped aside (or didn't). He saw the Devil was useful if you didn't look at him.

####

Once there was an old man who had seven sons he loved very much. They grew up and the oldest said, "Father, it's time for us to marry. Give us our horses and provisions so we may go out into the world and seek our fortune."

"Oh," said their father. "I couldn't bear for you all to go. I couldn't stand that. If you must go, let the youngest, Boots, stay here with me."

It was agreed. Their father suited up the boys with his best horses, clothes and gear.

Didn't they look a sight with their tack and provisions! If you had seen them coming from afar, their brilliance would have blinded you. They journeyed into the great world.

Boots stayed with his father. They waited for the boys to return, the brothers, the sons, the anticipated men, the hoped-for women. But the longer they waited, the more the brothers didn't come. The old man worried and cried, cried and worried. Finally, Boots said, "Father, let me go find them."

"Oh no, my boy, I could never do that. What if I lost you too? My dearest son, that would be too painful. I could not go on living if that happened."

"But I'll come back."

"Besides, I've given my good horses. There's only Old Groaner."

Boots bade his father goodbye and set out. "I'll bring them home," he said. Old Groaner was not as fancy a horse as his brothers had rode away on, but Boots was glad to have a horse.

Boots journeyed near and far, seeing the world from a different perspective from that of his brothers. His clothes and gear were as motley and tumbledown as his horse, and people paid little attention. As he rode old Groaner down the dry and dusty road, he chanced to see a fish which somehow had flipped itself out of a lake. Boots was tempted to build a fire right there and eat it— it would extend his food rations, which consisted of a small roast beef sandwich-- one more day; but he saw it was still breathing, and he decided his desire to see it keep living was greater than his hunger at that particular moment. So he got off his horse. The fish seemed to say, "Throw me back in the water, please." And that's what he did. He got back on Old Groaner and moved on.

They rode some more at a slow pace, seeing what there was to see, which was a great deal, even if it did not include what Boots was looking for. They were well past the reservoir and coming into the woods when Boots saw a black shape by a tree stump. As they came closer, he saw what he thought was a dead raven⬚ an odd sight, he thought, you don't usually see ravens die out in the open. To his surprise, the raven uttered a deep croak. If you have ever heard a raven utter, you know they are very expressive. This raven may as well have said straight out, "I'm hungry," because that's clearly what he intended. Boots was moved and got off his horse. He took his sandwich out of his satchel.

"I don't have much," he said. "But I'll split this with you." He broke the sandwich in two and gave half to the raven. The bird took some of the sandwich in his beak and stood upright. He ate some more and his feathers grew lustrous. When he finished his part of the sandwich he seemed to have grown in size, opening his wings to prepare for flight.

Boots felt stronger just watching him fly away.

That day was a long one, partly because Boots was still hungry after eating half the sandwich, but also because every town he stopped in, no one had seen his brothers, nor heard a thing about them. The sun was low in the sky when he saw something in the middle of the road. Approaching, he saw a wolf stretched across the path, even more withered and shrunken than Old Groaner, looking at him imploringly.

Boots got off his horse. "I'm very sorry for your situation, but there's really nothing to be done. I shared the only food I had with a raven a while back. I have nothing for myself even. I'm sorry."

The wolf's eyes shifted to Old Groaner. "No! I'm not giving you my horse! He's all I have. Absolutely not!"

And a palpable intelligence from the wolf's eyes glowed as if to say, There is a world you need to master.

Some people would have thought the wolf was trying to save her own skin. But Boots had a different hunger, and a promise to keep.

Not at all sure he was doing the right thing, Boots lifted the bridle and saddle and blanket off his faithful horse, and led him over to the wolf, who promptly leaped on him and ate him. Boots didn't watch the gruesome carnage, but looked around for material to build a fire, for he imagined that was where he would spend the night, before continuing on foot in the morning. But when he came back, the wolf was waiting for him.

She looked much bigger than she had before, now nourished and sated. She seemed to have actually doubled in size, beckoning for Boots to climb on. For the second time, Boots did a thing which went against everything he thought or believed, because it felt right: he climbed onto the back of a wolf. When the animal beneath him took off running, it all seemed natural.

They were covering ground. It almost felt like they were flying. Boots couldn't guess how far they had gone, but it was dusk when they came to a hillside, and the wolf stopped as if to say, Look. There were figures on an otherwise bare hillside. Boots approached, thinking, Are these statues? It seemed a strange place for an open air exhibition. What's more, the statues were remarkably lifelike. It was as if they had been captured in the moment of movement, so real did they look. For a second, he thought of his brothers, but there were too many of them. Then he came closer and saw that they were his brothers, and with them, women⬚ and one man⬚ on the hillside, frozen solid in varying expressions of fear and panic, a demonic sideshow that would have made him insane were it not for the steadying, calming influence he felt coming from the wolf, who stood and watched it all.

Boots saw a door eight feet high built into the hillside. He knocked on the door, no response; it wasn't locked so he opened it. There was a young woman sewing by candlelight in the rear of a windowless room. When she saw him, she gave a deep sigh and said, "Who are you?"

Boots said, "I am brother to those outside on your lawn."

"I'm sorry to hear that. You'll be joining them as soon as the Giant who lives here comes back."

"Well, I'm here to recover them after all."

"You can't kill him. He has no heart in his body. There's nothing there."

"He has it somewhere. Would you help me?" They were silent. "Maybe you would like to be free of him too."

Her expression changed from one of pity to amusement. "Well, I guess if you must, you must." Her voice changed as her eyes looked away. "Get under my bed fast!"

Boots scrambled to get under a long sturdy bed in the corner. It wasn't long before he heard the door open and a voice heavy with the weight of the world say, "What's that smell?"

"Oh, hello, Dear. How was your day? What smell?"

"I smell a man. A Christian man. Was there one here?"

"There's been no man here. It's probably some bones a buzzard dropped down the chimney. Are you hungry?"

Everything became quiet for a while. Boots heard the clink of dishes and utensils and pictured them eating. That is, he pictured her eating. He didn't want to think of what the Giant looked like. Although he hadn't eaten much that day, he didn't think about food. He put all his mind and intention into staying quiet. After a while he felt the mattress above him sink, and was glad it was firm. There was some movement and then stillness, and Boots thought they were going to sleep when he heard her say, "You know, sweetheart, there's one thing I would like to know."

"What?"

"Oh, where you keep your heart."

"Why do you want to know that?"

"It would be a special place to me."

"Huh! I keep it under the doorway, if you must know," he said as he turned over.

We'll see about that, thought Boots.

The next morning, the Giant got up early and was gone. As soon as Boots heard the door close, he said, "Is it all right?"

"Wait five minutes," she said. When he came out she had already pulled the carpet away. She handed him a shovel and a sharp-pointed spade and he was digging.

It wasn't easy⬜ the hillside was more rock than soil⬜ and Boots dug until his calluses bled. Then she said, "He was lying. We'll have to put everything back." Boots filled the dirt back in, and the young woman went out and picked flowers, cut garlands, tied ribbons and wound vines around the doorway.

When the Giant came back after dark, Boots was under the bed. "Has there a Christian man been here by any chance?"

"Oh, hello Dear, are you hungry? Man? What makes you think such a thing?"

"I can smell him."

"Oh, you know how powerful your sense of smell is. That was a bone a raven dropped down the chimney. I tried to fumigate the house, but you have a such a powerful olfactory sense."

"Hm. Yesterday you said it was a buzzard."

"Buzzard, vulture, raven, I don't know. One of those birds that eats dead things."

After they had gone to bed, the Giant said, "Why did you fancy up the door?"

"Well, that's where your heart is, you know. It's a special place to me now."

"Huh. It's not there. You think I'd tell you where it was?"

"Oh. But I would really like to know." There was a long silence.

"Okay. I'll tell you. It's under the pantry."

We'll see about that, thought Boots. And as great as the Giant's raw force seemed to fill the house embedded in the hill, he wondered at the bravery and the cunning of the young woman, and he hoped she wasn't married.

The Giant left the next morning and they pulled out all the pots and pans, skillets, ironware, griddles, grates, trays, and forks, and they started to dig. They dug till noon, and she said, "He's told another one." So they spent all afternoon putting everything back and decorating with wreathes, ribbon, spangles, pinecones and garlands, tinsel and glitter and glitz. It was pleasant doing that with her, Boots forgot it was getting late and had to hustle when he heard the Giant coming back.

There wasn't much time between Boots getting under the bed and the Giant saying, "Hmm, I smell something."

"What do you smell, Dear?"

"There's a man been here."

"No. I wouldn't let a man in here. You smell a man's bones. Some carrion-eating bird probably dropped a bone through the chimney. I've told you before you need to put a hood on it. You can smell the way an eagle can see."

"Oh. Why all the finery, frills and frippery over the pantry?"

"Well, you know, you told me that's where your heart is. So I wanted to honor that place."

After they had dinner, they went to bed.

"Fool. I would never tell a woman where my heart is. You will never know that."

There were low murmurings and rustlings of sheets and covers and many indecipherable sounds, like waves rolling back upon themselves, or leaves caught in a gentle whirlwind. Boots listened as intently as he could. Finally he heard her say, "I just can't help wondering. It's the one thing I would so like to know."

Boots heard the Giant give a long sigh, and when he spoke his tone had changed. His voice was calm and steady and slow and grave, as if he spoke of something both inevitable and inexplicable. His sentences came with long pauses in between.

He spoke as if in response to the silence she had brought him.

"Far, far from here, there is a thick woods with no path in between the trees. Not even a bluebird could fly through. In those woods there is a lake with an island in the middle of it. An island that is connected to nothing, yet goes nowhere. Sheer stone slabs surround it. On that island is a church. In that church is a well. In that well swims a duck. In that duck is an

egg. In that egg... in that egg is my heart, my darling!"

We'll see about that, thought Boots.

The Giant left slowly the next morning, and Boots grew anxious, waiting. He had to break away from that house he'd spent three nights in, and from the young woman.

"I'll be back," he said after the Giant had finally left. She looked as if she did not see the sources of his confidence.

As soon as Boots stepped out the door, the wolf was waiting. It was a strange mission they were on: looking for someone's heart whom he had never seen. He did not ask the wolf what the Giant looked like because he didn't want to know.

It didn't take long, such was the speed at which they almost flew, skimming the trees like a squirrel. Soon they were through the woods and at the edge of a lake, at the center of which they could see the island. The wolf stopped at the water's edge. Boots swam. Upon reaching land, he clambered up massive blocks of granite strewn with firethorn. The ground at the top was level. The island was small, the church in the center, its windows boarded up. Two wooden doors were closed and locked. Over them was a key on a nail twenty feet off the ground. He turned to look at the wolf and held his palms up. The wolf just looked at him. Oh, yes. The raven.

"Raven, I need you!" There he was, lifting the key in his beak, then dropping it into Boots' cupped hands.

He fitted it into the door and pulled it open. Inside was a musty smell. He approached a well in the center of the nave, and looked into it. There was a duck swimming around in a circle. How long have you been here, he wondered. He held out his hands and she came to him. As he lifted her out of the well, she laid an egg, which promptly sank. The duck flew out the door. This time, he didn't have to look at the wolf. As he thought fish, the fish he had seen on the road appeared, dove and resurfaced with the egg in his mouth.

Boots took the egg and the left the dark church. The island was all rock, the sun warmed it. Boots held the egg up so the wolf could see it. What to do? The wolf slowly shook her head. Boots closed his hand around the egg. He could feel a pulsing. He gave it a gentle squeeze.

A cry of agony from the other side of the world filled the air. Set my brothers and their sweethearts free, Boots said to his hand that had the egg in its grasp. Boots looked up at the wolf, who was nodding her head. "And every living thing you've turned to stone," he said quietly, and counted to four. Then Boots squeezed quickly with all his strength.

It was then that day turned night and back to day, and to night again. The earth shook. A searing scream cut across time and space, a jagged rusty blade of movement that sounded like the undercarriage of the firmament, causing everything to flash and shake three times and ring, as if all creation were a glass bell in pain.

Then everything was gone: egg, church, island, wolf. He was back on the hillside, a brilliant sun shining down, and his brothers were walking toward him, and the others; and the young woman coming out of the hill. And there was a laying on of hands, and a grand feast.

About the Author:

Bill Pruitt is a fiction writer, storyteller, poet, and Assistant Editor with Narrative Magazine. His short stories appear in recent issues of Crack of the Spine Literary Magazine, Indiana Voice Journal, Midway Crack of the Spine Literary Magazine, Indiana Voice Journal, Midway and Hypertext. He has published poems in such places as Ploughshares, Anderbo.com, Off Course, Stone Boat, Otis Nebula, Literary Juice, Visitant and Cottonwood. He has two chapbooks with White Pine and FootHills; and the self-published Walking Home from the Eastman House. He has performed his original story, "Two Kinds of Fear," a documented telling of the lives of Susan B. Anthony and Frederick Douglass at various venues in Rochester. He taught English to non-native speakers for 26 years. He and his wife Pam live in Rochester and have a daughter, a son and two grandchildren.

WHITE FLAG

by Jesse Kemmerer

Bootsie had been washing dishes in the kitchen when he first saw it – a white piece of something tied to a tree in the woods behind the house. It had been an unseasonally long winter for Blacktop, West Virginia standards, and though they were now venturing further into spring, the trees were still bleak and dead-looking, standing stiffly in a sea of brown leaves. Except for the white something flapping in the wind, sticking out like snow in summertime, nothing in that barren expanse of wood moved.

"Hey Momma!" he called, scrubbing the last bit of muck off a frying pan.

"Huh? What'd ya say?" she called back. She was in the living room, not twenty feet away.

Bootsie sighed and turned off the water. He leaned his elbows on the countertop and buried his face in his hands. "Momma!" he yelled, the word coming out muffled but loud all the same.

She'd heard him this time. Her cane clicked against the linoleum as she hobbled into the kitchen, signifying her arrival. Bootsie wiped the exasperation from his face.

"What? What are ya yellin for?" she asked. She was a small woman, and hard. She looked to be all bone underneath her sweater. Her short black hair stuck to her scalp as if it were a hair net.

"I think the trees is givin up," Bootsie said, pointing out the window.

She didn't say anything, only stood there looking at her son with a wild expression.

Bootsie took her by one bony hand, guiding her to the sink. She seemed to shrink into herself at his touch. He pointed at the white something flapping through the tree line. "See?" he said. "It's the trees – they's given up." He squeezed his momma's shoulders and smiled at her.

For a moment, she didn't say anything. It was if her son were some foreigner on the other end of the telephone line when you called about your credit card or hospital bill – she couldn't understand a word he was saying. "What are ya flappin your gums about?" she asked.

Bootsie felt his cheeks get hot. "They's flyin the white flag," he said, by way of explanation. He again pointed at the white something flapping in the wind, as if that would clear everything up.

She was awe-struck. Her mouth hung open, the shade of her lipstick making a perfectly red O like a bullet-hole where her mouth should be. "Are you dumb or something?" she asked. She shook her head as if she already knew the answer. Before her son could respond, she reached up and slapped a fragile hand across his face. It landed like a ghost from beatings' past – all the shame but none of the sting. She shouldered him away and hobbled back into the living room, muttering under her breath about stupid sons and their stupid notions, her cane clacking along the linoleum, punctuating each word.

Bootsie watched her go, feeling his cheeks redden as if he were ten years old again. He turned the water back on and finished washing and drying the dishes, looking up at the white something blowing in the trees every so often just to make sure it was still there.

Though he was 46 at the time, Bootsie didn't have much say when the decision was made for him to move back in with his momma, who was edging into her mid-seventies and required in-home care. He was the most likely candidate to look after her.

She'd chased the last three day-nurses out of her house with a broom, if Mrs. Kinneson, the nosy neighbor from next door, was to be believed. Stowing her away in a nursing home was out of the question. Big Jim, the eldest brother of the family and the only one moderately well-off, certainly wasn't going to foot the bill, not when the rest of his family – his younger brother Kurt, who fixed transmissions at Dale's Auto when he wasn't fixing himself with moonshine the night before; his younger sister Irene, who was living off food stamps with her deadbeat boyfriend; and baby of the family, Bootsie, who'd lived on couches and futons for the better part of his life – weren't able to chip in. "Besides," Big Jim said the night they were all gathered around his dinner table, discussing what to do with their momma when she was released – or thrown out – from the hospital, "Momma wouldn't last two weeks in a home. She'd sneak whiskey in somehow and get on one of her mean streaks, bitin other patients – er, residents, I guess – and smackin nurses' ankles with her cane. She'd get the boot and then we'd all be right back where we are now, only a couple thousand bucks lighter."

Bootsie smirked. Not at the thought of all 97 frail pounds of his Momma stone-drunk, terrorizing a nursing home with her oak cane; he smirked because he knew Big Jim was about to make a decision for the family. That's the only time his accent ever came out.

"So I was thinkin, Boot," Big Jim said, crossing his legs and resting his hands on his knee as if he were about to give one of his employees some bad news – Sorry, bub, but I'm gonna need you to come in at 6AM every weekend for the rest of your life. "Why don't you move back in, take up your old room? You'll have a hell of a lot more space, and you can keep an eye on Momma, help her up the stairs, make sure she's takin all her pills and washing them down with more than just licker."

Bootsie wasn't thrilled about the idea, but at the time, he couldn't think of a reason to say no. He was living in Irene's attic on a futon that was roughly half the size of his body. He wouldn't mind being able to spread out in a real bed at night. And besides, someone had to look after Momma, who was currently in the hospital after having her second fall in three weeks. Luckily, her nosy neighbor, Mrs. Kinneson, had dropped by and found her lying motionless on the floor. If she hadn't been there to call 9-1-1, Momma might never have woken up. Bootsie didn't know if that was necessarily a bad thing – he had no warm and fuzzy feelings for his momma, who was collectively despised throughout the family – but he thought she deserved a better end than seizing and foaming at the mouth on her living room floor. "I s'pose I could," he said finally. "For a while, at least."

Their father had died ten years earlier of renal cancer, and Momma had been living on her own ever since, save the three failed experiments of hiring day nurses to look after her. The house never seemed to have left the mourning stage after his death – the blinds were perpetually closed, every room shrouded in a heavy darkness that was further punctuated by brown carpeting, wood-paneled walls and plastic-covered furniture. Momma, on the other hand, seemed to thrive in the role of bereaved widow; she was seen in bars and thrift stores around town for years after wearing all black, telling anyone who'd listen what a fine man her husband had been. "He went out with his boots on," she'd say, wiping an imaginary tear from the corner of her eye. That was a lie, of course - her husband had gone out on his back in a hospital bed, his skin so yellow and jaundiced that he looked more like a rotten zucchini than a human being – but it racked up enough sympathy points to get her an extra five or ten bucks as she hawked his baseball card collection or commendation medals from the Navy.

Everyone in the family expected her to put the house on the market after the funeral, though they didn't expect to see one red cent of the profits (they'd been told as much before their father even passed). It was an old house, built sometime in the early fifties. It sat on a considerable chunk of land – there was grass to be mowed and trees to be trimmed and other general maintenance needed done to keep up the property. It was clearly no home for a widow in the last years of her life, and the family told her as much. Big Jim even offered to pay the deposit on a small, one-story apartment for her, figuring it would be cheaper than paying a landscaping crew to come out once a week for the next however many years until she finally croaked, but Momma held on to the house like a miser. "I'll die here 'fore I sell one square inch," she said when her son broached the subject, pointing a bony finger at him. "And don't you forget it."

The family kept up with their visits and the yard work for a while, but as the seasons rolled by, they found it easier and easier to come up with excuses. Big Jim had to work. Kurt was too sick (in Kurt-parlance, that meant hungover). Irene once made the mistake of having her new boyfriend of the month, Trayvon, a six-foot-five black man with hands that could probably palm a fully inflated beach ball, drop her off one Saturday morning. Momma had been on the porch, rocking in her chair with her morning coffee, which she took black with two dashes of Jack. When she saw the Cadillac pull up and saw that Nubian Adonis kiss her one and only daughter on the lips, she threw her mug at the windshield. It landed in the grass well short of its target, but then she grabbed the shotgun from the house, aimed at the car with two shaky arms, and fired. The gun didn't go off – she'd never thought to check if it was loaded when she'd grabbed it from her late-husband's bureau – but the intended effect was achieved; the Cadillac sped down the road, and Irene never came back.

Bootsie stopped by the least, and by the time he moved in, he hadn't seen the house or his momma in nearly two years. He found that both had grown markedly older and more decrepit; his momma wobbled more heavily on her cane, shaking it as if it were a magic eight ball every time she put it down (Bootsie secretly hoped for the time it showed up BETTER LUCK NEXT TIME), and the grass and weeds

had grown lush and jungle-like around the house, swallowing it up. Every window was closed, curtained, and possibly even boarded up, or so it had looked to Bootsie as he stood in the driveway with his bags in his hands. The house showed no sign of life; not even a memory of one.

The new living arrangement took some adjusting to, but Bootsie and his momma got along about as well as they could throughout the years. It was a fairly large house – three bedrooms, two baths, with an attic and dirt floor basement – and they used the space well, avoiding one another as a snake avoids a mongoose. They were rarely in the same room together, dinner being the one exception, which Momma always had on the table at 5PM sharp. If there was any redeeming quality about her, it was that she made a mean supper, always home-cooked and greasy and filling.

Bootsie helped her up the stairs, into the shower, even off the commode, on a handful of mutually embarrassing occasions. He set her pills out for her every morning, noon and night. There was no speaking between them during these times, and afterwards, there was no acknowledgement that any help had been either given or received; it was a simple nurse-patient relationship.

He tried to keep up with things around the house by himself, but eventually figured them a lost cause. He found that no matter how many weeds he rooted, more grew back within the week. They'd been allowed to fester too long, he decided one day, and gave up altogether.

As for money, the social security checks Momma received were enough to get by on. Bootsie worked odd jobs a few times a week as he'd done his whole adult life – a little carpentry here, some auto work there. He would splurge sometimes on nice cuts of steak or chicken from the butcher. Momma always fried them up special, and they would both enjoy the meal silently.

Life rolled by that way for a long time – silently.

Now, five years later, a week after Bootsie saw the white something flapping in the wind, he stood in front of the sink, washing and drying dishes. The window was open, a hint of spring whispering its way into the small kitchen.

He was fifty-one years old, now. The top of his head was bald, the sides lined with stubborn clumps of thin, graying hair. He wore the same pair of overalls he'd been wearing for thirty years, with a t-shirt underneath that held three days' worth of stank and stench. He'd inherited his daddy's potbelly in his old age, and he couldn't remember the last time he saw his prick. Hell, he couldn't remember the last time it had been touched by more than his hand. Still, that hint of spring – of life – permeated through the kitchen for the first time in years, it seemed, and Bootsie thought it was a damn fine night to be alive.

He looked out at the trees in the woods, searching for the white something he'd seen flapping in the wind a week ago. It was hard to tell if it was there or not - so many of the trees already had white blossoms of their own. He didn't think it was.

"Hey Momma!" he called.

He wanted to tell her about the trees, how they'd decided not to give up after all. Then he remembered that she wouldn't be able to hear him upstairs in her bedroom.

And besides, she was dead.

Bootsie's nephew, Jimmy, stood at the top of the attic steps with his hands shoved deep in his pockets. His shoulders were slumped, his head lowered in a posture of utter defeat, partly because the cross-beams at the top of the attic stairs were less than an inch above his head but mostly due to the sheer volume of junk that surrounded him on all sides. "We're never gonna finish," he told his uncle.

Bootsie sighed and sat on one of the many boxes lining the walls. It sank under his considerable weight. "Aw, hell. We'll make a dent, won't we?"

Jimmy kicked around some dust. "Not a big one," he said, looking more downtrodden than ever. He hoped his uncle would just agree with him. The attic looked to be a makeshift dump - there was no way they'd be able to clean it all up in one day.

His uncle said, "Put your mask on, son." A gust of wind blew and the house groaned, taking the sentiment right out of Jimmy's mouth.

After an hour, they hadn't made much progress. Boxes and decorations and newspapers and furniture - all the junk that seems to live exclusively in rickety attics across America – littered the small space, everything old and musty, coated in a thin layer of dust, grimy to the touch. For a while, Jimmy lugged trash bag after trash bag down the steps and out to the curb, trudging back up to the attic a few minutes later red in the face and huffing through the dust mask around his nose and mouth, clumps of sweaty hair sticking to his forehead. Then, Bootsie had an idea. He opened the window at the far end of the attic and punched the screen out. "Hand me a bag," he said, then tossed it straight out the window. It landed on the lawn with a crash. They waited, silent as the bats that were still hiding undisturbed in whatever corners of the attic they had not yet reached, then Bootsie said with a sly smile, "Hand me another one."

Subsequent trash vacated the attic much quicker. Boosie saw his nephew's face light up every time he threw something two stories down and watched it crash and break apart on the lawn. After another hour and two-dozen more tosses out the window, they went outside to arrange the trash pile for pickup.

Bootsie watched from the porch sipping from a mug of sweat tea while his nephew dutifully swept the trash from the lawn and piled it onto a growing heap by the curb. It was a beautiful spring day – the first warm one of the season – and it had come in like a lion; yesterday morning, you could feel winter in your bones, but today was spring, by-God, and you could feel it in your heart. Birds were chirping in trees already starting to bloom, a noon-day sun provided warmth and light to everything beneath it, and the smell of life was in the air, fragrant the way it can only be in those first days of spring, before your nose becomes accustomed to its scent, forgets its even there. As Bootsie sat on the porch sipping his tea, watching his nephew muscle trash bags and boxes into piles that kept toppling over, he thought that it was a damn fine day to be alive.

"You got it, son," he said when the last of the trash was squared away on the curb. "Come take a rest."

Jimmy walked up to the porch wiping the sweat from his forehead. His white t shirt was dirt- and muck-stained, clinging to his body in wet patches of sweat. He sat heavily in a rocking chair beside his uncle.

"You done good today," Bootsie said.

"Thanks Uncle Bootsie," Jimmy replied. He cheery now, happy that the day's work was done before lunchtime.

"Are you hungry?" Bootsie asked.

"No," Jimmy lied. His stomach grumbled and they both had a laugh.

Bootsie knew why his nephew didn't want to have lunch, and frankly, he didn't blame him. As if reading his thoughts, Jimmy asked, "Why is she so mean?"

It took courage for him to ask something like that, Bootsie knew. He watched his nephew's face redden, saw his eyes drop in embarrassment. "That's just the way she is," he said.

"But why? What did anyone ever do to her?"

Bootsie clapped him on the back. "No tellin," he said, and that was the end of it.

Jimmy's father pulled into the driveway a few minutes later. He'd recently bought a new truck — a ford F-150 with chrome rims and a slick blue paint job. He climbed out of the cab in his suit and tie, traced his fingers across the hood, pausing for a second to lick his thumb and wipe away a smudge or stain that was most certainly not there.

"Hiya Big Jim," Bootsie said when he walked up the porch steps.

"Hey Boot," Big Jim said absently, then turned to his son. "Get some work done today?"

"Yessir," Jimmy replied.

Big Jim eyed his younger brother sitting in his rocking chair. He asked him the same question.

"Aw, we did all right. Another pass or two and we'll have it licked," Bootsie said.

Big Jim seemed to consider this, perhaps thinking if history were any indication, that second or third pass would never come. "Let's go say 'bye' to Grandma," he said to his son.

"She's takin a nap," Bootsie said. He made a drinking gesture, holding his thumb out and tilting it towards his lips. Then he reached into his back pocket for his bill fold.

"That's not necessary," Big Jim said, but Bootsie plucked a twenty out anyway and handed it to his nephew. "Good work today," he said.

Big Jim gave him a look. "Really, Boot, we don't need your money."

"Aint no we about it," Bootsie said, ruffling his nephew's hair. "You got yourself a good worker here."

Big Jim nodded.

"What do you say, son? Same time next week?" Bootsie asked.

Jimmy's eyes flicked over to his father, who was looking perhaps more intently at Bootsie than he should have been. Aint no son a yours, those eyes said, in the same accent Big Jim had had for twenty years or more, before he moved to the city and got a job slinging papers instead of asphalt. He nodded, and Jimmy nodded, too, sticking his hand out to his uncle. When Bootsie shook it, he pretended his hand was being crushed by his nephew's grip, yelping and slapping his knee, begging him to lighten up. Jimmy giggled, then gave him a hug.

Big Jim took his son by the shoulder and they got in the truck and drove away. Bootsie watched the dust billow out from behind the truck's big back tires, hoping at least a little bit of it managed to stick to the paintjob.

###

A week later, Big Jim dropped his son off at the house. Bootsie met his nephew at the door.

"Hey Uncle Bootsie," Jimmy said, wiping sleep from his eyes. "Yard looks good. What's with all the open wi – " He scrunched his face into a ball and dry heaved, his tongue sticking out and his eyes bugging from their sockets.

Bootsie placed a dust mask around his nose and mouth, the same kind he was currently wearing. "Sewer line busted," he said, explaining why every window in the house was open. That was a lie, of course; the source of the stench was his momma's decomposing body.

"Gramma's probably havin a cow," Jimmy said.

Bootsie laughed. "I'm sure she is," he said, and led his nephew up to the attic.

Jimmy couldn't believe his eyes – or his luck. The attic had already been cleaned, for the most part; all the trash and various odds and ends had been put into trash bags, anything heavy had been lugged downstairs, and even the floorboards were free of dust, the yellowish brown of the wood shining in the morning sunlight coming through the window.

Bootsie saw the smile on his nephew's face. "We got 'er licked, now," he said.

It didn't take long for them to finish up. Bootsie had already done most of the legwork, and by the time the last of the trash was thrown out the attic window, it was only 10 o' clock. Jimmy sat indian-style in the empty room, looking around in awe. A week ago, the space had been nothing more than a trash heap, and today all that was left was a cumbersome vanity mirror and a bag of his Gramma's old hats. "We did good, Uncle Bootsie," he said. His uncle sat down beside him. "Yessir, we did," he said.

They were silent for a time, both of them sitting cross-legged on the bare attic floor. Jimmy started scratching one of the floorboards with his fingernail. "About last week, what I said about Gramma," he started. Bootsie let him find the words himself, looking at him blankly. "I didn't mean to call her mean," Jimmy continued. "I know that's not a nice thing to say, specially about your elders."

"She scares you a little, don't she?" Bootsie asked.

Jimmy looked at his uncle wide-eyed, shaking his head. "One time, I was standing a little too close to the fan, so she – "

Bootsie put his hand up and his nephew sputtered off, red in the face. They both knew the story and they both knew there were countless more to tell.

"I just don't get it," Jimmy blurted out. "Why don't we just let her... I mean, why does anyone even come around to help anymore? Why do you have to live with her?"

Bootsie considered this for a while. Then he said, "Do you remember your Grandpappy?"

"Not really. I know he got sick."

"Uh huh, he did," Bootsie said. "But before he was sick – before you were even thought of, youngin – he bought this house for your gramma. He was twenty-five or so then, and he'd squirreled away enough take-home pay from the Navy and from workin odd jobs when he got back stateside to put half down on it, cash. He paid the rest off over a ten-year span, not a single nickel coming from nobody else."

Bootsie could tell the weight of what he'd just said was lost on his nephew, who was all of eleven years old, but he went on regardless: "This was their – your gramma and grandpappy's – home, and it was mine, too, same as your Daddy and your Ant 'Rene and your Uncle Kurt."

Jimmy eyes darted around the room, unsure what to settle on.

"Now, your daddy might wonder why your Gramma decided to hold on to in her old age – you mighta heard him sayin as much to your momma around the dinner table. He mighta thought she'd take the money and move into a home or an apartment, but he's not seein things from her point of view. Our daddy bought this house for us, not nobody else, and your Gramma wasn't about to spit on that. She wasn't about to let go of it til she was dead in the ground beside him."

Jimmy nodded his head dutifully, and Bootsie nodded back.

"Point I'm tryin to make," Bootsie said, "Is ain't nobody all-good or all-bad, ain't nobody all-right or all-wrong. You ask why your Gramma is so mean all the time – and she is mean, I know it as well as anybody – but you forget she's lived seven lifetimes more than you. You forget she's old and cranky and alone." He sighed.

"We didn't have much love for her as kids, your daddy least of all, and we don't have much love for her now. But I think we all have a little. She raised us, after all, she's our Momma. And just 'cause you don't like someone, that doesn't mean you shouldn't try to do right by em."

"Uncle Bootsie, you're, uh...," Jimmy stuttered. He looked plainly uncomfortable, still chewing away at the floorboard with his fingernail, avoiding eye-contact with his uncle altogether. "Do you want me to get you a tissue or something?"

Bootsie reached up and found wetness in the corner of his eye. He wiped it away. "Come on," he said, "there's some work yet to be done outside."

When Big Jim pulled his truck into the driveway a few hours later, Bootsie and Jimmy were raking up freshly mown grass, piling it into big contractor bags and dumping them into the woods behind the house. Big Jim lent a hand.

"How'd he do today?" he asked his brother.

"Hard worker, that son a yours," Bootsie said, beaming at his nephew. "Fine young man you got there."

"I'll tell you, Boot," Big Jim said just as the last of the grass was being picked up, "Place looks good. Damn good. I didn't know you'd planned on cleanin up, else I woulda stayed and helped. Hell, it looks like it did when we was kids."

"Like I said," Boosie replied, ruffling his nephew's hair. "You raised yourself a hard worker."

Big Jim nodded. "I got some papers for Momma to sign," he said, going to his truck. He handled all her finances, big city man that he was.

"She's nappin," Bootsie said weakly, but Big Jim was already making his way inside. Bootsie shoved his hands in his overall pockets and followed, telling his nephew to stay outside and keep an eye on his daddy's truck.

Big Jim almost ran right back out the front door, but Bootsie was there blocking it. "What the hell is that smell?" he asked, coughing. Bootsie pointed upstairs. "In her bedroom," he said, pulling a dust mask from his pocket.

You're gonna wanna wear this." He handed it over.

The look on Big Jim's face was a mixture of confusion, horror and revulsion. By the time he opened the door to his momma's bedroom, it had leveled out into cold understanding. "Christ, Boot," he said, closing the door just as quickly as he'd opened it. "How long's she been in there?"

"Week or so," Bootsie said. He'd hung a dozen car air fresheners – the evergreen scented ones – around the room trying to mask the smell. He'd pulled the covers over her face.

"And you didn't think to call nobody?" Big Jim asked.

Bootsie shrugged his shoulders. "Weren't ready yet," he said, unsure if he was talking about himself, his momma, or the house.

Big Jim pulled out his cell phone and dialed the only numbers he could think to dial: 9-1-1.

###

Bootsie hadn't killed his momma, of course, but he was charged with Failure to Report her death, which carried a $500 fine. He had to borrow the money from Big Jim.

Death had taken Momma peacefully in her sleep, he later learned from the coroner's report. Respiratory failure. She'd simply stopped breathing at some point in the night, and never started back up again. Bootsie accepted that fact, though he didn't much believe it; he couldn't imagine his momma being taken peacefully by anything.

He stood on the other side of the street with Mrs. Kinneson, the nosy neighbor, as they rolled her body out. He thought he'd done about the best he could. The paint was still chipped in places – it needed a fresh coat about ten years ago - and the bones of the old house still sagged onto its foundation, but the lawn was cut and the weeds plucked and the windows open, letting light shine through. Standing there looking at it, Bootsie thought the house might even harbor some life between the floorboards.

Or at the very least, a memory of it.

OUR BILLY

by Tom Lakin

First, we found out what had happened. "Did you hear?" we asked, across marble countertops and in oak-paneled studies and through the open windows of cars, morning cold pouring in and turning our breath to steam. "Can you believe it?" we said as we pushed piled carts across the grocery store parking lot, voices raised to be heard over the tinny jangling of the small black wheels. "How awful," we whispered into telephones, lips wet, our breath hot on the mouthpiece.

At the dry cleaners, our pressed, plastic-wrapped suits swaying like headless ghosts on the conveyor, we shook when we heard and coughed into nervous hands. Passing beneath the fluttering awnings of Main Street, we clutched arms and traded soft, sorrowful looks. In the dens and living rooms of our fine cherished homes▨ Victorians and Tudors, Dutch Colonials with broad gambrel roofs▨ we wondered how such a thing could happen, could possibly have come to pass, in a good town like ours. This is a bright, pleasant place▨ a family town. Our children ride bicycles down safe, shaded streets; most mornings they walk to school. To pass through our town is to hear the whirr of polished cars, shouted greetings, collars jingling around the glossy necks of Labrador retrievers: happy sounds, safe sounds. In spring, handsome flags snap from porches and we wash our cars in the drive. Holidays are taken seriously here: on Halloween, jack-o-lanterns guard our doorways and cardboard skeletons dance from the branches of our trees, thrilling costumed children and startling neighborhood dogs. At Christmas, we gather before bay windows and watch the snow fall like bits of torn paper onto the lawn.

And yet there we were, receiving this news on playing fields and in church, outside coffee shops and in line at Brown's Sporting Goods, sneakers and brand new footballs in paper bags at our sides. We heard it from neighbors hurrying uneasily up our long, curving drives. Some of us were out of town when we heard it, and the distance▨ the miles of unfamiliar road or the roar of the city or all that sky beneath the steel belly of the plane▨ dulled the news and made it feel somehow less than real, vague and disembodied, and yet all the more horrible for being so plainly, so coldly, a matter, now, of permanent town record: that young Billy Wilson was dead.

THAT EVENING, we held a vigil at the football field. It was cold, and we huddled in tight clusters by the goalposts, blowing into our hands and stamping our feet in the snowcrust. Beneath our boots the frost crunched and popped, and our breath was like steam in the darkness. Nearby, a streetlamp gave off an eerie glow, and the air was clear and bright with the smell of snow. Behind the old wooden bleachers thin threads of ice tinseled the heavy branches of the trees. Someone had brought candles, and we lit them and passed them carefully along rows of shaking hands. Their flames danced and threw strange shadows on our reddened cheeks.

When the silence became too much to bear, we began to talk▨ about the cold, about Billy. "I remember last fall, against Oldham, when Billy scored five touchdowns in the game's first half," we said. "We'll never see anything like that again." "And the Landry scrimmage!" we whooped. "Billy threw that damn ball fifty yards in the air and the Landry kids were looking up as it sailed past like it was some kind of UFO, and then down it came, gentle as a balloon, into Harper's outstretched hands. Touchdown, game won. Boy, that was some kind of pass." No one mentioned what we all knew: that they'd found Billy's body in the high school locker room, hanging from a ceiling pipe near the showers. Being a captain he'd been given a key to the gym, and we were told he'd snuck in after hours and done it, but not before returning his helmet to the equipment closet and hanging his uniform neatly in his locker. An assistant coach, come to collect a late student activities fee, had discovered him swinging there in the dark.

We all knew Billy⬚ we'd watched him soar down the field, our cheerleaders had designed special dances for him, the paper had acclaimed his name⬚ but few had spent much time with him, it seemed. He was seventeen but appeared much older in uniform, his face slim and unlined beneath his helmet, the cloth chinstrap biting into the dimpled flesh of his chin. Off the field he wore glasses and played classical piano. He did well in school, though he sat in the back of the classroom and hardly ever raised his hand. It was said that he enjoyed woodcarving, would spend hours at it long into the night after practice and games, and that his bedroom, which few had seen, was dotted with little figurines: soldiers and cowboys and tiny fisherman casting matchstick poles. He lived in a small brick house on the north side of town, facing a busy street, and he had a younger brother named Mike. His father worked as a football coach at a local college and his mother, a tall, cheerful woman with long reddish hair, stayed home.

On weekends, though Billy would appear now and again at parties, floating quietly among pockets of indulgent classmates, he was never wild, and nobody ever saw him drink much more than a beer. He existed for us, then, primarily in box scores and in the block text of headlined feats: the Lincoln game⬚ three rushing touchdowns and two more in the air⬚ or the time he intercepted a pass thrown by the legendary Whiz Ellington and ran it ninety-three yards for a score. Whiz threw his helmet to the ground as Billy sped past, and the photo

in the paper that week showed Whiz standing there with his mouth wrenched open and his eyes aimed at the sky, and Billy just a streaking gray blur at the edge of the frame. The photo hung on the wall at Center Deli, by the register, its corners going curled and yellow with humidity, and its image is the one we carried of him in our minds: a comet-tail flashing unknowably through our town.

It was strange then, we thought, that photos of his familiar, inscrutable face should now decorate the snow at our feet, where we'd placed them at the base of the goalpost among other tokens of Billy: flowers and footballs and piano-shaped key chains and a tiny peewee football jersey, number nineteen⬚ Billy's number. Someone had fashioned a cross out of branches and stuck it in the snow, and a piled shrine had grown around it. There were candles and balloons, flags and small football figurines. A framed picture of Billy⬚ his senior photo, a posed shot in which he grinned at the camera with his broad chin resting on folded hands⬚ lay at the base of the cross, and beside it a pair of white sneakers glowed like unblinking eyes amid the snow-light and the brilliant glitter of crushed ice. As we stood there, surrounded by these Billy-things, our hands joined and our skin scorched with cold, already we could feel the face in the pictures hardening into something symbolic. From the snow Billy stared back at us, and behind the glasses we saw the stone eyes of a statue, and on his face a monument's frozen grin.

After a while, someone began to sing: a hushed "Amazing Grace" that seemed to emerge out of the cold itself, out of the wind and the hard-packed snow. Quickly we took up the song, the words rising like smoke from our mouths before vanishing above the pointed tops of the pines. For what felt like hours we stood there singing, the candles flickering in our hands, though probably it only lasted a minute or two, or even just a handful of seconds⬚ it was impossible to tell. At some point in the night, time had excused itself, had disappeared into the darkness and the cold, and there was no way to know how long we'd been standing there or when it would be time to leave. Finally, after the song's last note had been sung, the first of us drifted quietly away, and, taking that as a kind of permission, the rest soon followed. We blew out our candles and took a last hard look at the boyish face in the pictures, and then we moved in a line past the goalpost and up the small rise of a hill, away from the trees and the still-burning candles, back toward the lights of town.

THAT NIGHT we dreamt about Billy. We saw him barking out commands in the backfield, eyes wide behind his facemask. We felt the slap of the snapped ball. We saw him flash past the line of scrimmage, dart around a tackle and hurdle a fallen linebacker, his feet throwing up chunks of sod. We saw the painted white lines of the field strobing by beneath his cleats. Then we saw Billy in a blazer and slacks up on the broad high school stage, seated behind a shining black piano, his head bowed over the instrument and those long fingers spidery on the keys and his pant cuffs rising now and again to reveal a seam of white sock. We saw him at his desk in an imagined bedroom, bent over a wooden figurine, his knife sending crescents of shaved wood into the half-light. Then abruptly those scenes vanished, the tinkling piano replaced by dark and cold, and we saw Billy swaying from a damp pipe in the locker room, a folding chair toppled beneath him, no helmet or blazer now and his neck bent at an unnatural angle and his arms hanging limp at his sides, the life gone out of him and on his face not the glasses or the old familiar grin but rather the faces of our own sons and daughters, the bright open faces of our children who we realized then were no longer safe here, in town, on the bus, behind their desks at school. They could be taken from us, run down by a madman in a speeding car, yanked sleeping from their beds. They were vulnerable here, now, because of Billy, because of what he'd done. We woke then, sheets soaked through with sweat, to the knowledge that our lives, our town, our very idea of ourselves had been altered in some vital, unrecoverable way.

THE NEXT MORNING, a Monday, arrived listlessly and cold♦ normal enough for the season, but with the sense that something had been knocked askew. In town, cars crept along Main Street toward the high school, their exhaust like the foggy breath of horses in the cold wintertime air, and shop owners shoveled crusted snow from brick sidewalks and wiped ice from their tall glass doors. Lights were coming on at Center Deli, and the mailman could be seen hurrying in and out of his small square truck. Overhead, the sky was scribbled with gray clouds. Along the roadside, wind shook ice from heavy pine branches and scattered it like diamonds across the hoods of our cars.

Sluggishly we went about our errands, fumbling change and dropping letters into the wrong mail slots, so fervent were our thoughts about Billy. There was fear in our voices now, a sinister quality that seemed to have crept in overnight. Had Billy been depressed? we wondered in low tones. Was he on some kind of drugs? It didn't fit with our image of him, but neither did his suicide fit with the safe, solid idea we had of our town. At first we'd accepted it as a freak, unexplainable thing, but now, in line at Chip's Bakery, we theorized that maybe he had been fighting with his girlfriend recently♦ hadn't there been a girl there, last night at the vigil? A slim blonde in a pea coat crying loudly into her mittens? Or maybe he'd been rejected from a favorite college, Middlebury, perhaps, or Tufts, somewhere the coach had assured him he'd get in. We knew how horrible that could be, such a blow. Our town took such care with our children's applications. We hired essay consultants and SAT tutors, paid slim men in spectacles hundreds of dollars to coach our kids through algebra and analogies. To be kept from a college of one's choice was a shameful, intimate thing, rarely talked about directly, though of course there were always rumors. Still, though, Billy was a smart kid, we knew, and moreover he was talented. We'd all seen him out there on the field, flashing past tacklers and somersaulting into the end zone for a score. We'd sung his praises, cheered his young name! His picture hung on shop walls; we saw his face each time we ordered sandwiches at the deli. Old men sat in shirtsleeves at Demos Diner and told stories about his feats, their sour breath like a gas in the brown half-lit gloom. He'd been somebody here, Billy had, a great glittering fixture of the town. His greatness reflected our own, and for that we loved him, and he us. Hadn't that been enough?

IN THE AFTERNOON, we drove furtively past Billy's house, slowing down as we approached the small brick colonial with its black shutters and gabled roof. The blinds were drawn over the windows, and there were several unfamiliar cars in the driveway. We saw no sign of the parents or of Billy's brother Mike, but we could imagine them huddled inside, dressed in black, rocking in armchairs or crying softly into balled tissues. We wondered about Billy's father, Brian, a large, stoic man with broad hairy arms and his son's dimpled chin. We remembered him pacing the sidelines at football games, a rolled program stuffed into the back pocket of his jeans and his hands pounding like gunfire when Billy dropped back to pass. "Good play," he would bark after first downs. "Good play now. Okay, here we go." It was all we ever heard him say. Did a man like that cry? Did he weep, there in the darkened house? We tried, but couldn't picture it.

And what about Maryanne, his wife? How had she gotten the news? We imagined a young police officer coming timidly up the drive, hat in hand, his legs heavy with what felt like sand. At the door he'd collect himself before giving it a firm knock. "Mrs. Wilson?" he'd say when it swung open, and the small robed woman behind the door would look at him with sleepy, fearful eyes and say, in a soft voice, "Yes? I'm Mrs. Wilson," and when the young man spoke again her face would go gray with shock. What had she done then? we wondered, driving past the shuttered house with its drawn windows and snow-covered hedge. What would we have done, given the same terrible news? We couldn't fathom it, and so we drove on, sped up and turned onto Route 9 and joined the course of our town's other fine cars toward home.

THE WHOLE TOWN turned out that night for Billy's wake. The line to get in snaked all the way down the block, past the police station and St. John's school and right up to the entrance of our old town hall, the last of us cast in shadow beneath its spired, gothic frame. The weather had warmed during the day, and we stood coatless in blazers and black dresses, chatting softly and kicking slush from the toes of uncomfortable shoes. Snowmelt fell from the leaves of trees lining the sidewalk and glistened in our hair. From time to time a good

friend of Billy's would drift past our line, and we regarded them with a kind of wonder, their nearness to tragedy having elevated them in our eyes to an almost supernatural esteem. There was something thrilling about their wretchedness, something attractive and singular, and quietly, standing there in our neckties and heels, we envied it. They had been touched by this monumental thing that had dealt us only a glancing blow, and we wished that we too could participate in the glamor of their grief.

Inside, the funeral home resembled a series of Victorian sitting rooms. Flowered armchairs lined the walls, interspersed with poster-sized photos of Billy that had been backed with foam and mounted on plastic easels. His smiling eyes appraised us as we shuffled past. The windows were hung with heavy cream drapes, their tops curved and pleated like bunting, and hunting scenes in gilt frames loomed above the fireplace. Light blazed from table lamps and from fine brass sconces perched at intervals along the walls, all of it washing the room in a hot, overbright gleam. Passing through the foyer and into the large main room, we could feel sweat beginning to gather in our collars and in the creases behind our knees.

The Wilsons stood in a line along one wall, Mr. Wilson wearing a blocky black suit and his wife beside him in a small cap with a fluttery mesh veil. Mike stood to their left, browned wrists visible below his sport coat sleeves, and next to him was a row of unfamiliar black-clad relatives, clasping hands and snuffling into handkerchiefs. Beyond them all, at the head of the room, hard against the wall and between two enormous bouquets of red and white roses, we saw the coffin, a black shining box with silver struts laid upon a broad wooden pedestal. Its lid had been opened halfway to reveal a silk-lined underside and another row of roses along its hinge, their faces like bright fists of blood against the field of sparkling white. Inside, propped against a silk pillow, lay Billy, his head back and his arms crossed at the waist.

They'd dressed him in a crisp white shirt and blazer, and around his neck was a tie dotted with little pianos. A small silver cross on a beaded chain had been laid over his shoulder, and a wooden ornament⬜ a tiny, unpainted solider⬜ nestled at his side. His face was not the one we'd just seen on the posters. It was a waxen thing, pale and strangely smooth, his skin the texture of crayon. His eyes were closed and his hair had been neatly combed, and where it parted the skin of his scalp was perfectly white. He wore a high collar and you couldn't see much of his neck. We had trouble looking at him: the sickly sweet smell of the flowers was overwhelming, and the glare of the lamps brought beads of sweat to the soft skin above our lips. Quickly, we coughed into our hands and moved along, joining the line waiting to speak with the Wilsons.

"Thank you so much for coming," Mr. Wilson muttered in a flat voice, his eyes aimed at the empty wall. "It means so much to all of us to have you here." His hand was clammy and cold. Mrs. Wilson had vanished, leaving behind her hat and a litter of tissues, and Mike filled her place beside his father. He was somber but composed⬜ dignified, we thought, as we watched him give firm handshakes and offer thanks for supporting his family. We knew him primarily as Billy's little brother, a freshman to Billy's senior, and we never envied him the task of following his brother in school⬜ certainly not now, after what had happened. Mike was a good football player in his own right, perhaps even faster than Billy, but small in stature and possessing none of Billy's strangely adult elegance. They were different people, we knew. Mike was a fixture in houses across town, and for three years running he'd sold the most tickets for our town's famed pancake breakfast, held each spring on behalf of the rotary club. You could count on seeing him behind a card table outside Fred's Grocery on Saturday mornings, calling out greetings and waving fistfuls of red stubs like a fine ladies' fan. Mothers were fond of him. He was a nice kid, we all said, and as we shook his offered palm there beneath the glare of the funeral home lamps, we wondered what would become of him now that his brother was gone. It was the kind of thing that could send a boy's train off the rails, we knew, and, even now we realized we'd begun viewing him differently, tracking his grief from a safe, kindly remove. This year we would buy too many tickets at his table and laugh too heartily at his jokes. He would move among us like a

well-liked leper, kept at arm's length by the stink of his tragedy, and soon, quietly, almost imperceptibly, he would be cast from the everyday life of the town. Knowing this, and believing in its rightness, in the naturalness of its truth, we patted Mike on his slender shoulder, bade Mr. Wilson goodbye, and hurried down the sidewalk to our cars.

WE ARRIVED EARLY the next morning for Billy's funeral, the ladies in long dresses and the men in trim black suits. The high school had offered to hold the service in the gymnasium because of the expected turnout, and our footfalls rang like small explosions as we tracked across the court's parquet floor. Neat rows of folding chairs stretched from baseline to baseline, and wooden bleachers had been pulled from the walls and raised to provide seating for the overflow. There was a makeshift altar on a portable stage beneath one basket, with a podium for speakers and an enormous video screen hanging from the ceiling behind it. A large white cloth lay on the floor in front of the stage, and atop it was Billy's closed coffin, its black sides gleaming like the painted hull of a fine sloop. Light streamed from high windows and made brilliant white squares on the hardwood. Everywhere was the smell of talcum powder and perfume.

We took our seats beside neighbors and friends, dabbing our faces with tissues and sweating into the waistbands of our underwear. Soon the Wilsons appeared and processed in a long black line toward the altar. We strained forward to watch their faces as they came. Mr. Wilson's was pale and dry; Mike's long lashes were pearled with tears. Mrs. Wilson came last, and we held our breath as she moved up the row of chairs, for it was her we most wanted to see. She wore a floor-length coat, belted at the waist, and her eyes were hidden by large black sunglasses. Her face⬜ strangely, we thought⬜ was utterly void of expression. She seemed to glide across the hardwood floor, touching nothing, making no audible sound. It was as if she had resolved not to offer us the satisfaction of her visible grief, and, disappointed, we sagged back in our seats and turned our eyes to the altar, where the pastor, a silver-haired man in a heavy black robe, was clearing his throat to speak.

"As we gather here today," he began, "we are shocked and angered by the senselessness▢ the unfairness▢ of our beloved Billy's death. Why has this happened, we wonder? What possible reason could there be for such an awful thing as this?"

In a lilting voice he went on, imploring us to remember Billy not with fury or rage, but with empathy for his struggles and wonder at the magnificent burst of his short life. The pastor closed with the Lord's Prayer, then he gently shut his Bible and swept down from the stage.

In the brief silence, the gym rang with the sounds of sniffling and sharp echoing coughs. Near the front a blonde▢ the one we'd taken to be Billy's girlfriend▢ sobbed loudly, nearly pornographic in her grief, her keening like the glittering screech of an out-of-tune trombone. Only when Mr. Wilson stepped to the podium did she quiet down.

His tie was loose at the neck, and he gripped the altar with two large hands. Flanking him on the stage were the same easled photos from Billy's wake: Billy in his football jersey, smiling up at something just outside the frame; a plump toddler Billy dressed as an astronaut on Halloween; Billy at prom, arms wrapped around the gowned waist of the blonde. "I look at these pictures, the recent ones," Mr. Wilson began in a hoarse voice, gesturing at the easels, "and when Billy should have been smiling I see only a half-smile. I wish I had noticed it sooner. I wish he had told me that something was wrong. I wish▢ " He broke down then, his voice dissolving into sobs, and Mike rushed to the podium and held out an arm and guided him down from the stage.

We heard little of Mike's speech, for the podium's microphone started sparking with static and someone scurried up to switch it off. He seemed solemn and serene, collected▢ the Mike we remembered from the ticket booth and the wake. He said he looked forward to playing in Billy's honor the following season▢ he would wear his brother's number nineteen. When he said this, his mother shifted in her seat and coughed into a black-gloved hand.

AFTER a piano-led hymn, Mrs. Wilson stood and walked deliberately toward the stage. Her steps were firm, her heels clacking loudly on the gleaming floor. A gasp rose from our seats: we hadn't expected her to speak. She stopped before she reached the stage steps, turned, and went to stand beside the coffin.

"None of you knew my Billy," she said, hands curled into fists at her sides. We snapped back in our chairs, faces flushed with disbelief. She used no microphone, yet her voice rang like a struck gong clear to the top rows of the stands. "Not one of you knew him. Not really. You clipped his photos from the paper and shouted his name, but you didn't know him. He hated football. I bet you didn't know that, did you? He was sick of it▢ football this, football that, my husband's football playbooks all over the house. He hated it, but he played it for all of you. Every day he wanted to quit, but how could he? How could he stop?" The words rushed out of her in a tumbling stream, each one a tiny detonation in the silent gym.

"He liked to read," she went on, crying now, black streaks on her face. "He wrote stories and funny little poems. He was good to his brother, he was Mikey's best friend. Isn't that right, honey? He loved Mike. He loved playing his piano and carving those little wooden figurines. He loved school, and he loved watching the seasons change, how the snow looked in winter and all the new smells in spring. He loved this town. He truly did."

She paused then, and her face grew hard. She'd stopped crying. "He loved it," she said, her eyes passing over the bleachers and the folded metal seats, "but this town took him from me. It stole him. You stole my precious boy."

With that she turned and laid a soft hand upon the coffin, then she gathered herself to full height, strode down the court's baseline, pushed through the double doors, and vanished out into the day.

IN THE DAYS and weeks after the funeral, we hardly saw the Wilsons around town. When we did encounter them, at the grocery store or coming out of church, we lowered our eyes and hurried quickly past. Forced to speak to them, we did so in soft, distant tones. Their tragedy seemed to trail them like a fog, and we did our best to stay clear of it. Nobody had any idea what to make of Mrs. Wilson's wild speech. She'd gone mad with grief, it was said; Billy's death had sunk her. The gist of it we ignored⬚ she hadn't made any sense, after all. Billy hated football? Impossible. He was a hero, an idol. We'd loved him, and in turn he'd loved us. They buried him in a cemetery in town, beneath a maple tree at the crest of a gentle hill. From time to time we visited, and placed toy footballs at the base of his stone.

In time, our town healed itself like the sea after a storm. By summer, people once again smiled and waved from porches, and hydrangeas decorated our lawns. In the fall, new stars emerged to race downfield for touchdowns, and at Center Deli, new photos were taped up on the walls. The high school band played loud as ever on the sidelines, and our old men found other things to talk about in their red booth at Demos Diner.

At some point we heard that the Wilsons had moved. Nobody saw them go; one day their house was simply empty, the curtains drawn and a For Sale sign posted in the yard. A few weeks later another family moved in, a young couple with shiny new cars and their own small children, two towheaded boys, who were soon seen scampering across the grass.

Sometimes now, on fragrant fall days, when the air is clear and a breeze sends leaves sailing from the trees, we'll think of the Wilsons and wonder where they've gone. To the city perhaps, or to the sea. Are they happy there? we'll ask ourselves. Have they found something we lack? But of course this cannot be, and so we'll shake our heads, bemused, and drift back down the streets of our fine, treasured town, its windows incandescent, our lawns like quilts of finest silk, all of it shining and unblemished and washed in golden light.

About the Author:

Tom Lakin is a graduate of Emerson College's MFA program, where he was a full-tuition fellow. His fiction has appeared or is forthcoming in Noble / Gas Quarterly, Lunch Ticket, Pleiades, Pembroke Magazine, and The Adroit Journal. He is the recipient of the 2018 G.B. Crump Prize in Experimental Fiction, and was a finalist in Narrative Magazine's Spring 2014 Story Contest. He lives with his wife, daughter, and Boston terrier in Boston's South End.

DROP OUT

by Raymond Tatten

A lazy ceiling fan coaxed May morning air past a wall portrait of President LBJ and through the crowded room as two marines looked up from clerk-sized desks.

"Tatten? Major Williams is expecting you. Go right in."

The major was tall, a middle-aged, athletic-looking man with hair burned close to his scalp, commanding a large wooden desk – clean of paper, as if no more than an affectation.

He leaned, reaching into the desk drawer for my letter.

"Help me understand; what's going on here?"

"I've decided to drop out; I'm not going back."

"You're six weeks from flight school. I thought you wanted to be a pilot?"

"I did. But everything's different."

The major pushed forward on his elbows.

"You're a top recruit, Tatten. Quantico said sixth in 600 – perfect fitness score."

The room stayed quiet with much unsaid.

"You know we need you, Tatten. The country needs you. Why don't you give this a little more thought?"

"I have...I've thought about it a lot."

The major held my eyes for long moments until the tension finally broke when he dropped his gaze and leaned back a bit as if comforting himself while preparing another attempt.

"You know, son... in thirty years, I've never lost a candidate to an opt-out. You'd be the first to quit."

I said I was sorry, but I wasn't. He had asked to see me, and I'd come. But I didn't give a damn about his perfect recruitment record.

"All right," he said, "I think we're done. See Sargent Wright for the paperwork."

I did not know, could not know, I would not speak of the meeting for fifty years – leaving a dream behind is private.

But when regret comes for me, I'm armed, recalling the image of a little Vietnamese girl running naked, her clothes burned away by napalm, protected with knowing horror had never rained from a plane I had flown.

About the Author:

Raymond Tatten is a life-long New Englander whose work includes numerous personal essays and articles published in The Bolton Independent, Meetinghouse News, Harvard Press, The Landmark, MUSED Literary Review and The Worcester Telegram. Current projects include an historical ficton account primarily for the YA reader, as well as a memoristic novel for the middle-school reader. Raymond participates in classes, workshops and critique groups with the Seven Bridge Writers' Collaborative in Lancaster, MA. and GrubStreet in Boston, MA.

THE VISITS

by David Massey

They drove deeper into the country, up and down hills, through pine and scrub forests on both sides of the highway, until they came to the dirt road that left the highway across from the country general store. As always, they talked but little, although he told Dorothy how much he liked Paul, his favorite uncle. She listened quietly, but in her manner was the reserve and calm thrill of anticipation that always came over her when she was embarking on anything new with him. By the side of the road rose clay hillsides; the road had been cut out of this clay. He wondered what his wife was thinking as they continued along in the midst of hardscrabble farms. He wondered what she thought of the countryside and of the probable life that people lived here; what she was anticipating was in his wonder, yet he knew she would not tell him. Other than explanations of what they ought to do in practical affairs, she never told him her thoughts except as terse enlightenment. These moments came in social situations, usually in a single sentence, as if she begrudged him the words; though but seventeen, she always knew the meaning of people's conduct, while he would stroll blithely through social landmines until they exploded. He thought he had a more catholic understanding than Dorothy, but her reserve gave him the uneasy feeling that she believed herself his superior. He wished she would be more forthcoming with him. His young wife seemed to him one of the most insular of people (although he had often heard her talking unreservedly with others, even men she hardly knew; taking candy from strangers, as it were).

They were not expected; Lee had just decided to drop in on his uncle as he had done a number of times before (and as he often did at the homes of his friends). Lee got out and walked around the car to open the door for Dorothy. She liked this chivalry. As they turned to walk toward the side door into the kitchen, she passed her right hand lightly onto his arm. She had taught him this etiquette.

When Sarah opened the door to them, her face flushed. "Lee!" she said. "And this is your wife!"

"Sarah, my wife Dorothy. Dorothy, this is my Aunt Sarah."

The two women greeted one another cordially. They seemed to like one another. Sarah, who was cooking, invited Lee and Dorothy to seat themselves at the kitchen table. Lee held Dorothy's chair for her, then sat on the opposite side of the table.

"Paul is in the bedroom," Sarah said. "He'll be right out. Would you like anything to drink?"

"Only some water, thank you," Dorothy said.

"Yes," Lee said.

Sarah poured two glasses of ice water from a pitcher. At that moment, the door at the end of the room swung open and Paul appeared. Something came over Dorothy – rigidness, fright, anger. Paul, who beamed upon seeing Lee, gazed at Dorothy in wonderment. "Hello!" he said. "Lee and his young wife! I'm so delighted to see you!" He came quickly toward them holding out his hand to shake Dorothy's, but she held her hands close to her body on the edge of the tabletop, leaning away from him, at once livid and frightened. Paul recovered from his brief discomfiture and sat at the end of the table.

"Well, this is wonderful," he said. "Where are you from, darling?"

"Roperville."

"Roperville. Yes. I went to Roperville once. I was looking for used farm equipment. I went to a farmhouse where some had been advertised, but when I knocked on the front door, nobody answered. I thought the people might be in the back yard, so I walked around the house, and there was this little girl. – She was dancing." He paused and looked hard at Dorothy. She leaned away, face frozen. "Anyway, I enjoyed myself tremendously that day."

He waited but Dorothy said nothing. "Well, that's my story about Roperville," he said, getting up. "I'll be back in a minute. I've got to take care of some things." He left through the door he had come in through.

Dorothy immediately leaned toward Lee and hissed in a whisper that he could hear but Sarah probably could not, "I want to go!"

He resisted. Turning toward Sarah, he said, "Is Paul farming full time now? I notice all his fields look cultivated."

"Yes, he loves it." She turned her back on her guests to take care of her cooking. Dorothy kicked Lee under the table. "I want to leave," she hissed.

"Why?" he whispered.

"I don't like him." She bit off each word, her whole person rigid, fury in her eyes and the pallor of her face.

"Why?"

She kicked him again. "I want to go now!"

It would be futile to resist. He raised his voice and said, "Sarah, we've got to go."

"Now? You just got here," Sarah said. "Don't go. Stay and eat with us."

"We can't. We're in a hurry. We just dropped by for a minute."

Dorothy was already on her feet. "Yes, we've got to go," she said.

The door at the end of the room swung open and Paul reappeared. He saw they were leaving.

"You're not leaving already?" he said. "You've got to stay for dinner. We're having pork chops and mashed potatoes."

"They have to go," Sarah said.

"We're in a hurry," Lee said.

As Paul protested, Lee put his hand on his wife's back and streered her out the door and toward the car. Paul followed, objecting. At that moment, crying, "Oh!" Dorothy put her hand to her ear.

"What's the matter, baby?" Lee said.

"It stung me," she said.

"Did you get stung by a yellow jacket?" Paul said. "There's a yellow jacket nest in that tree – I've been meaning to get rid of it, I should have gotten rid of it. Let me see that, dear."

"It's all right," Dorothy said, sorely vexed. "It's nothing."

"Where did it get you?" Paul said.

"It's nothing."

"I think it got her behind her ear," Lee said.

"Let me put some tobacco on that," Paul said. "That will draw the poison out."

"That's not necessary," Dorothy said.

"You can't go running off like this," Paul insisted. "Just wait here for a second while I get some tobacco."

She resigned herself. He came back with tobacco and put it on the sting wound and put adhesive tape over the tobacco to hold it in place. She endured his ministrations, Lee felt, with an ill grace. He glanced at Paul anxiously to see if he was offended.

"There. That will draw out the poison," Paul said.

Lee thanked him and he and Dorothy said their goodbyes. In the car, in what he knew was a wounded voice, he said, "Why didn't you like him?"

"I just don't," she said through a clenched jaw. They said nothing of moment the rest of the way home. They passed an unquiet evening and went to bed dissatisfied with one another.

Next morning at 7:30 Dorothy went off to work and Lee was left to ponder the visit to Uncle Paul. He got ready for work and at about noon sauntered out of the apartment. When he was a few paces from his car, he was amazed to see Uncle Paul crossing the street toward him. Paul seemed disappointed to see him but covered his feelings in a show of bonhomie.

"Where are you going?" Lee said.

"I was coming to see you."

"I'm leaving for work."

"Is Dorothy home?"

"No, she's at work."

"That's too bad. I did hope we could get over our little misunderstanding of yesterday. Well, maybe I'll come back."

He did not know how to respond. He could not say Dorothy would be glad to see Paul because she clearly would not. They exchanged a few more words and Paul left.

Lee was distressed by Paul's visit but decided to suppress thoughts of it. He went to work and had a hard day at the factory. That evening he told Dorothy of Paul's visit and the hint that he might come back. Dorothy exploded in fury, "He'd better not show up at this door. I'll call the police!"

Lee looked at her in bafflement. Her actions appeared unaccountable. What had Paul ever done to her? But she often did things he did not understand and would not explain herself to him. Once when he complained that she did not try to understand him, she said, "I believe I do understand you. And don't you think a marriage should be a two-way street?" When he asked what she meant, she said, "Never mind. You wouldn't comprehend." He was stung, but could get nothing else out of her. Now he saw he could not be Paul's nephew as long as he was married to Dorothy. But why can't I? he thought. Then there came knocking at the back door of his mind an awful connection between his uncle and his wife. He drew back in horror. He did not want to see what such a thing had to do with Dorothy and Paul. He decided the best thing for his peace of mind was to forget he had ever thought of it.

He did not know if Paul ever came back.

About the Author:

David Massey has a Masters Degree in English Literature After 1660 from The University of South Carolina and, while there, took creative writing classes under George Garrett and James Dickey. He turned rather belatedly to an earnest engagement with the craft of fiction but has made progress of late. In 2017 he had two short stories published and so far in 2018 has had a blog post on the craft of fiction published in Black Fox Literary Magazine.

RESTART

by Amada Matei

Restart. Reboot. Refresh. New day. Fresh start. Forget regrets. My therapist told me I needed to find a ritual to remind my inner demons that the past is gone and today I can start anew. Beat down the beast that gnaws at my past digressions, vexing regrets and silences my foreboding predictions of moral failures, all by lighting a candle, sitting cross-legged on the floor, eyes closed, and singing my mantra. What is done is done; it is what it is; let the past stay in the past. I think of every axiom that conveys self-forgiveness and hope and perhaps if I hum the incantation long enough and loud enough, the morose images in my mind's eye will pop like a pus-infested pimple. All my errors will ooze out and I will feel cleansed as if nothing ever happened. I will be reborn. Five minutes of humming and breathing and visualization turns into a laundry list of meetings, memos to write, dinner parties, and some ass kissing at the CEO's luncheon. It's a lukewarm attempt at Nirvana, but I got to start somewhere. New day. New chapter. Restart. All is forgotten.

I shave my face, remembering half way through that my work wife likes it when I'm scruffy, giving off a rogue vibe, yet still fashionably hip. Now it's too late. I shave the rest of me and jolt at the tiny dagger lacerating my chin. Blood cascades past my jowl and a wad of toilet paper is my only medical device. I stop the bleeding and get dressed in a crisp blue shirt, purple striped tie, and the rest of my underling uniform. I rub my hands together as if I'm washing them and take a deep breath. Count to four. Exhale. The ritual of soul cleansing is eating up my time. I grab my briefcase and start my day.

My first stop is the drive-thru for a caffeine buzz. "Three seventy-five," says the girl with the nose ring.

"That's a quarter more than usual," I say.

"Sorry. I don't set the prices."

With my overpriced latte in one hand, I veer back into traffic and jerk forward and back, forward and back, slamming on my brakes for the nitwit in front of me. Forward and back. I hit the brakes again, this time a dollop of hot coffee stains my lap as I curse the nitwit and the coffee and the traffic. I glance at my watch every two minutes as I crawl through the muck that is my life.

Thirty-five minutes later, I'm in my parking lot gripping the steering wheel like I'm wringing out a wet towel and breathing myself back to Earth. Restart. New day. Breath in and out. Count to four.

My boss visits my desk as soon as I sit down reminding me of our meeting, the one that's a regurgitation of our weekly flimflam, except this time I have to present to the big wigs. I head to the bathroom to dab and dry my pants while I recap my speech in my head. My monolog is perfect, everyone is fixated on my impeccable delivery, and verbose gobbledygook. My boss is awestruck, he shakes my hand at saving the company lots of moola, and insists I accept a raise and the corner office.

My reverie is shattered by my near collision with Margo as I step out into the hallway. We smile and do the tango to get out of each other's way. "Hey John. Aren't you in a hurry?" she says.

"Sorry. Got that damn meeting on my mind," I say and stare at her breasts. "Speaking of things on my mind, you given any thought to that drink?"

"About that. Not sure if it's a good idea to mess around with coworkers. I just don't want it to be awkward later. I hope you can understand that."

"Sure. No worries," I say remembering her last Facebook post showing off her long legs and low-cut sweater, clinking beers with that He-Man from IT. He was drooling over her exposed neckline and she appeared lit like a meandering firefly. Awkward, my ass.

I take the stairs, two at a time, stacks of manila folders nestled in the crux of my elbow. My asthma-like breathing gets shallower with every climb because I didn't realize three flights of stairs was the equivalent to Iron Man training.

A bunch of minions and ass kissers were spread around the conference table when I stumbled in, as beads of sweat clings to my hairline and I'm no longer confident in my antiperspirant. Count to four. Past mistakes stay in the past. Today stays in the present.

"John, we've been waiting. We all got lives to live," says my boss scribbling in his notebook, not bothering to look in my direction. "I hope you're ready."

"Absolutely. I apologize for being late." I plop my files onto the table. Stacks of paper slide out and ice skates towards my boss and bowls into his coffee cup. It topples over, spewing any remaining liquid onto the table, absorbed by my handouts. I don't dare check my boss' expression. I save what I can and accept napkins from an altruistic neighbor. No one says a word. I grab more paper towels by the donut platter at the front of the room. I dab the coffee cup dry and hand it to my boss.

His is stoic and his hands remain in his lap. "You can throw it out. I'm done with it now." I obey with clenched teeth and resume collecting my stained paperwork.

"I apologize everyone. This is not how I wanted to start this meeting, but at least my handouts will now offer you a free whiff of caffeine," I say with a chuckle but no one is laughing with me.

My fresh start is no longer fresh. It's no longer new. It smells like day-old coffee and body odor. I pass out clean copies to my coworkers and throw the wet ones in the recycling bin. The minions look bored, uninterested, impatient. A couple of people have to share a copy. I spew lackluster numbers, irrelevant facts, and monotonous figures.

A colleague questions part of the data. It's correct, I insist.

"No, it's not," she insists and digs deeper and I feel my penis shrinking with every debasing comment she makes. Then it's settled: my numbers are off and I leave the meeting a couple inches shorter.

The day is stale by noon. My heart feels like a thirty-pound organ suffocating every breath I take. It pumps acid through my veins. I heave into the toilet, expecting blood or bile or demon piss. My heart is beating a thousand beats per minute and another drumming heart appears in the middle of my brain. My therapist said panic attacks are a manifestation of the mind because it feels it is losing control, stuck in the corner with no way out. I breathe. I choke on my vomit before swallowing it back down.

I hear footsteps outside my stall, then they patter away minutes later. My tongue feels like sandpaper and my armpits are saturated with fear and the stench of embarrassment. The cell phone in my back pocket vibrates. I reach back to pull it out and land hard on my ass when I answer.

"John, where are you?" I recognize my work wife's voice.

"I'm in the bathroom stall, Second floor."

"You're having another attack, aren't you? Need me to call someone?"

"I'll be fine. I need a moment to find my self-respect."

"I heard about your meeting. A hot mess." She laughs like she feels sorry for me, but it makes me smile listening to her voice.

"I don't know what to do."

"You said you'll be fine."

"I lied."

"I'm coming to get you."

A few minutes later I hear her voice announcing her presence. "I'm a woman coming into the men's bathroom. If you have a dick, better cover it now!"
She hears me laughing and crying. "I thought I was going to die," I say when she crams herself into my stall and lifts me by the arm. "I'm supposed to be the man helping you dry your eyes, not the other way around."

"My life is finally getting to where it doesn't suck, and that's thanks to you holding me up. I'm returning the favor, so don't try to be macho."

"I'm glad I was useful. I wish my ex-wife thought of me the same way."

"Forget her. She had it made with you. She blew it."

"I hate my job. I despise my boss. I lost my wife. Everything I touch turns to shit."

"First, don't ever become a motivational speaker. Second, this is nothing a stiff drink can't cure."

"I'm going to make this up to you. How about I buy the drinks tomorrow night?"

"No way. You cry like a school girl," she says and I can't stop laughing. My heart calms and I can breathe. I wash my face and walk around the floor to relax my nerves and situate myself back at my desk.

Four hours later, I park my car in the garage. While listening to talk radio and the humming of the motor, the garage door descends and touches the threshold, sealing me in. Talks of the slowing economy and a surprise downturn of the S & P 500 dominates the news, but the journalist's lullaby voice makes it all sound so trite. I roll down the window and breathe. My eyes are closed. I think of new beginnings. A fresh start. The fumes waft towards my face and seep into my nostrils, my mouth, my ears, my brain.

My cell phone vibrates and sings. My work wife's photo appears on the screen. I smile knowing she cares about my wellbeing and perhaps knows me too well. I turn off the ignition and answer her. She calls to remind me that tomorrow I can start again. Reboot.

Restart.

About the Author:

Amada Matei works and lives in Cleveland, Ohio. She is a graduate of John Carroll University and holds a Masters in Sociology from Cleveland State University. By night, Amada supervises a child abuse hotline, and by day, she's writing her first novel. She has contributed other works to Adelaide Magazine and was a finalist in 2018 for the Adelaide Anthology short story contest.

THE KIND SOUL HE IS

by Barbara Bottner

"We're not putting Boomer down," says Dan, rushing after his morning shower. Our chocolate lab, Boomer, as if he were fluent in Death, sidles up to him, snuggles at his feet and gets Dan to scratch his neck. Why can't my guy see how it hurts Boomer to move? Why can't he see how exhausted he gets? If Boom could talk, he'd say, I can't do this. I need to rest. I'm ninety years-old. Pooped. Pooping constantly.

But Dan doesn't see a lot of things. He doesn't see me even if I'm planted in directly in front of him. Or if he does, I'm cast as the high school principal during after school detention. At least, that's what I think he thinks.

Boomer stares at Dan. I think our old guy might be crying. Dan stoops down and strokes him, coos to him. He's saying its okay, old boy. It's okay. I'm thinking, Dan, that juicy tenderness… can I have a taste?

I turn the radio to NPR and hear people discussing their work with Gorillas, who are so famous for nurturing their young. They groom their babies, inspect them, protect them. They don't bear an offspring and decide, that actually, they were too young at the time; it was the wrong move or maybe they'd be happier in advertising.

I have always been jealous of gorilla babies and those long hairy arms they use to encircle each other. Jealous, too, of certain women whose men stick around while they finish eating.

"Our dog's incontinent," I say.

"Boomer is still okay for awhile," Dan's picking out a shirt while I shower. "I don't want to move to Texas either," he says as if we're in the middle of that conversation. His communiqués just go booing! Pop tarts that fly out of the toaster. You have to act like a plate, ready to catch them.

 "How about this one?"

"I like it."

While I dry off, Dan holds up a tie that I bought him. It's our ritual. Easy to agree on a tie, a way to start the day that will have its own confusions, misunderstandings, disagreements. Marriage is like that. You cultivate certain rituals so that when things don't shake out, you can at least stand at the closet and agree on the red paisley tie.

My guy and I need every close encounter we can get. Things have been testy between us since Margareta, a head hunter, obsessively has been pitching Dan a radiology gig in Texas. Laredo Texas. At first he said no. But the money is calling to him. He says the hospital has great equipment. Besides, we'd live large, have cooks, maids, drivers, and we'd learn Spanish. I say it's not a place a Jewish woman who talks too fast, wears too much makeup and writes snarky comedy for even snarkier comedians could live. It's rural. If you own a cow I don't want to talk to you.

Call me intemperate. I don't care.

"I belong in LA," I tell him.

"Traffic," he answers.

I plead with him to turn this job down. To consider me. But he keeps having private conversations with Margareta. I hear him joking with her; she must be a real hoot.

So there's that hanging over us. And since Boomer's era of incontinence, we've been arguing about when exactly his exit should happen.

It has to. See, Dan insists on a pristine-clean home but he doesn't help in any way. I never signed up for months and months of cleaning up dog poop, even the poop of beloved Boomer. Before I met Dan, a doctor no less, I never saw myself as even remotely domestic. My moon is not in Venus or wherever the heck it should be when it comes to vacuuming.

Dan is oblivious about what makes a house a home. Being a Jewish Doctor and the son of a Jewish doctor and a nurse, he focuses on science and medicine: his observations about domestic life are not keen. He can't see newspapers on the floor or dishes in the sink. To him, a house is like a self-cleaning oven. I tell him I'm not a spray-on cleaner. Or a spray-on anything. I'm not an ambient wife.

He says 'oh, that's so funny.'

Last week, I finally met someone who understood.

This guy with an earring, Jim, was here last week to fix the icemaker in the refrigerator. He looked as if he'd lived hard and maybe had too many days at sea with too many bottles of Scotch. He was missing a prominent tooth. But he was a talker and I liked him. While I made a salad, he told me this sad story about Francine, his girlfriend, who had just died. Right off, he told me what he loved about her.

"She was such a good cleaner, man. The best! She was fantastic. When she left a place, it was entirely fucking sterilized. See this counter, he referred to the granite island in our kitchen, she'd move this counter if she could, and clean over it and under it, man," he said, swilling his second of Dan's Dos Equis. "There was nobody like this girl." Jim's green eyes locked mine to make sure I was getting his message As if I had a choice. He almost started crying.

Francine, this lady of Jim's. wasn't even his wife! I do this Wife Deal. I do it way too much. Before I was a wife, I was once so not wife, you could hardly get a cup of coffee off me. I was making art, chumming around with theater people, writing grants, discussing and perfecting the Work. But the very minute I became a spouse; the Collective Unconscious dropkicked into my brain. It was so sudden. It's like, now I almost care about dish soap. Ask me where to find the best Romano cheese. You go up Melrose near La Cienaga...I know about red peppers, marinades, carpet cleaners; I am a fluff and folder now, I swear I am.

But I'm not a pooper scooper. No. Can't do it.

Dan and I, we both need a Francine.

By the time I get into the kitchen, Dan's long gone. Only the intense Gevalia coffee aroma snitches that his getaway was made merely minutes ago. My next move is to see if Boomer might have extended his life by doing his morning poop outside. I gingerly look around corners and jubilantly discover Boomer has not, shit on the white tile floor. I compliment him while I fill his bowl and I and thank my lucky stars that I don't have to be a desperate housewife with dog shit today. But then, around the counter; on the far side of the refrigerator, I almost step on a familiar brown lump. Boomer hobbles away, embarrassed. Dog shame. My spirit falls to the floor like a damn boulder. Here I go again, searching for the paper towels, the plastic bag, the mop and bleach. How can you scold a pet that has no muscle control? Dan has made this point many times. While I finish cleaning everything up, I complain to the God who gave me a un-communicative husband and an incontinent dog.

I call Dan to give him the bad news, but he's in the recovery room with a patient. I hold until they finally put me through.

"Okay, then put him down already!" he shouts. "Just don't ask me about it!" Then I hear the intercom: 'Radiology... pick up line 3.' They don't even bother to use Dan's name; I know he has trouble with that. I wish he felt more appreciated at work. I was brought up to believe men wanted to conquer the world. Turns out, they mostly want someone to say 'nice job. Thank you. Good boy.'

And they want a treat.

No wonder Dan adores dogs.

I call the vet and make an appointment, then find Boomer's leash. With great effort he struggles to his feet, the spirit willing. I'm pretending this is our regular, occasional trot around the neighborhood. He's having trouble, so I follow along as he stumbles. Sits. Lies down. Tries to get up. So, we just go to the end of the property. It's refreshingly cool outside which makes my face tingle pleasantly. I love the feeling of air rushing into my lungs; it's as if life comes towards me, inviting out.

I complain to Boomer about the smell; he licks me like the kind soul he is, as if licking is something that makes me feel better. Typical male. He wants to hear \good job,' too. He limps, sniffs, earnestly trying to be the hearty pup he once was. Every once in awhile he barks; he can still bark. A cat, a rustle of a tree; Boomer is on duty, ruff ruff, that's my boy.

Back at the house, he pants, splayed on the floor, I talk doggie to him, brave Boomer, always taking care of his girl, Stormy. Thank you, you old guy. He wags his tail; he's so good-natured. We're very close, his innocence, my guilt.

I'm shaking but I have to face the fact that I can't live this way anymore. I can't start my day with the pungent smell and the clean up job. I leave a message on Dan's voice mail, requesting that he meet me at the vets after work. I cut up steak. Boomer only sniffs it, and then eyes me suspiciously which he does whenever I give him really good food. He only eats a few small pieces, and slowly. He must sense something; he never eats leisurely. But today he's a thousand chews a bite--a macrobiotic lab.

I pet him and brush him and notice how willing he is to cherished. Then I shoot a few parting shots; Boomer is all raised eyebrows. Even through the lens, though, there's no disguising his droopy skin and grey hair.

Boomer's old.

Now I'm all business, trying to get him inside the car. He works diligently to oblige: his hind legs are not able to hoist him up. I give him a boost. We work with each other, he wants to be spring into the seat, but he can't and I almost fall down under his weight.

What a spectacular day, as if Boomer himself picked it: the low humidity, the clear skies and temperatures in the high sixties. How lovely it is that the weather of our last moments on earth are perfect.

I lead him to the Toyota.

His eyes swivel; cameras snapping shots, his mouth dripping saliva, his tongue licking my arm as if I were doing him a favor, which is what the car represents to him. Trips, parks, an adventure. I heave in a breath. That was the wrong thing to do----breathe. I burst out in sobs, a river of apologies flood the car. I tell my dog how much I've loved him, and how I'm sorry I have to do this, and he's such a good, good dog, such a born comedian, and he's made us so happy. And remember the walk in the hills he loved so much, and the doggie park, and how he got the squirrel one night? And how he drank from my bidet thinking it was a doggie fountain? What about the year we dressed him up for our Christmas card; he was famous all over town. How he'd snore next to Dan and I could never make out for the life of me who snored louder. How he preferred certain lawns in the summer to roll on, and how we took him up to Oregon and he had two delirious weeks frolicking in the creeks and running thru the grass, his ears flying and how at night, he lay in front of the fire so tired and happy. What a funny little guy he used to be when we first rescued him. And then I'm pleading for his forgiveness, and soon, I can't even see the road in front of me, my eyes can't focus. I'm hysterical, heaving, sobbing, wailing, my heart is simply breaking open. Boomer regards me with avuncular concern as we pull off Ventura Boulevard into the vets' lot. I take the collar and hook it up to the leash and help him stumble out of the car onto the pavement.

He's immediately searching for life, as usual. Something interesting. His attitude is so completely positive; he doesn't need Louise Hay tapes or CD's of mindfulness meditations; I accept and love myself exactly the way I am.

In we go. The pretty Latina receptionist asks why we're here until she takes a look at my miserable face; then she hands me a Kleenex, nods and disappears.

Meanwhile Boomer is interested in the other dogs; he pulls on the leash, sniffing them. My God, his last moments on earth are so friendly, so sweet. I feel the collective Sadness of Ever Saying Goodbye to Love. I'm swallowing guttural sounds, hoping I'm not noticed, hoping nobody here know my mission. My Kleenex is useless. I need extra strength.

"I'm sorry, dear," says a frail woman with a poodle who she calls Finley. "He seems like a lovely pet." She reaches out to Boomer and he licks her in his dumb, enthusiastic way. Her poodle and Boomer sniff each other.

"Boomer's very last dog friend," I blurt out.

"I can see that, on your face, dear," she says kindly. "Finley likes him."

I wish she wasn't so nice. Nice hurts.

Boomer barks at Finley. Our old man wants to play. Come on, Finley, man. Play with Boom!

I continue to weep; tears plunk onto his fur. Now, Doc Rob, tall, a little furry, and possibly the most relaxed human I've ever met, opens the heavy door and signals me inside. I pull the leash and Boomer manages to rise. Inside we go directly to a steel and glass cubicle. Rob checks his file then explains how this is going to happen. It won't take long, only several minutes from when he injects. Boomer will be entirely comfortable. That stings me somehow. Shouldn't death be uncomfortable? Or maybe I'm thinking of life.

Doc Rob has an easier time getting Boomer on the table than I would have imagined. He has a talent for this. The doctor pets him and gently talks to him. Boomer only makes a few whiny sounds, but we are both so present, he must see our hearts. I try to quit my laments but it's no use. Who wouldn't weep? I can't stop myself from murmuring tenderly. I can't seem to shut up.

"This is the right thing to do," says Dr. Rob. "Ready?" He's not morbid or cold, just focused; there's a job to do. This helps me, too. He hands me a big white towel. I nod okay, but I'm not.

I think: I hope my demise will go a little like this, somebody that I love witnessing, connecting when it most matters. I don't want to be alone then. I don't want to be with an introvert like Dan, who might be busy scratching his leg while I die. I don't need to die insulted.

As the doctor loads the lethal stuff, I'm trying to hold on. I look into Boom's eyes, hum, coo, and try every utterance a human can make to soothe another sentient being. At some point the needle is inserted and Boom's eyes have begun to close. Slowly, they do fall shut. And then he is quiet. The doctor nods.

Boomer isn't here anymore.

It seems that every loss I've had, or maybe even the collective loss is now anchored in my gut, my shoulders, behind my eyes. My heart contracts like a fist. I'm buried in the white towel.

"Do you want to stay in the room for a minute?" Doctor Rob asks.

I shake my head yes. Then, no. No! Then, yes, please. I keep whispering stupid metaphysical stuff he'd never understand, like does he see the light as he passed, or his mommy? I make promises about how there will be new life in a brand new body; he'll be a fluffy, healthy, tail wagging, steak-fetching, tongue-licking pup who can run and sleep without snoring. The truth is that I'm waiting for that dog to get up off the table and come home with me. I want resurrection; not re-incarnation, which takes too long.

Then, I get up and run through the waiting room, past the doggies waiting for shots and teeth cleanings, over to the cashier. I struggle with my wallet, not able to look at her, aware my face is probably streaked with makeup.

"Why did I put on blush when it always runs? I knew where I was going," I say as I dig for my checkbook, which I can't find.

She says, don't worry, we'll mail this to you later. Do you want his ashes?

I shake my head yes, which strikes me as the wrong answer but she says they will drop them off for me in a day or so. I clear the door, dash to my car and collapse in the driver's seat. Dan is sitting in the passenger seat staring ahead.

"Why didn't you wait for me?" he asks testily.

I give him a disbelieving glance as I grab a tissue to try to get the thick mascara glunk off my face.

"I didn't think you'd come!"

I can't look him in the eyes because if he's even a little tender, I will tear apart like an old rag. So I look at my hands. Then at Dan's. Then at my hands gripping each other as if I squeeze them hard enough I won't wail.

Then I notice Dan's breathing. He's trying not to cry too.

"Dan, Doc Rob says he deserved to stop suffering. You always told me if you had to suffer too much, you'd want to die."

"Well, I'm a coward," he reminds me.

There isn't much more we can say. Dan inhales and exhales loudly. He's digging for a tissue and snorting so he doesn't have to blow his nose which would be, I guess, a confession of his sorrow. Finally his tears do emerge, slowly, as if even crying has to be restrained and dignified.

I adore him for this sadness---his sensitivity is probably why I married him.

"Honey…." I say tenderly.

"He was the best dog," bleats Dan.

"He adored you, honey," I mumble.

"Nobody will ever love me like Boomer loved me," he says gloomily.

"Excuse me!"

"You know what I mean."

"I'm fucking devoted to you; you realize that, don't you?"

"Sure, honey, but you're not a dog."

"Well, either are you a dog, Dan!"

He shrugs again.

"Okay, tell you what? I'll take that remark that I'm not a dog as a compliment," I say.

"I didn't actually mean it as a compliment."

"Well, Boomer loved me better than you do, any day, Dan."

"How can you say that? The long hours I work."

"I know you work long hours," I say gruffly.

"I suppose you'd like me to lick you when I get home?"

"Yes, actually," I admit. "Or do something friendly. Anything would be better than playing Solitaire on the computer with the focus of a Traffic Controller."

"I can't believe we're fighting over this," says Dan. "Boomer helped me relax after work."

"Maybe I could do that," I say. I begin crying again.

There's a Pancake House next door to the Vet's. We take a booth and use Maple Syrup to medicate our pain. The waitress must sense something; she talks so quietly I almost can't hear: do we want more coffee? Maybe she's used to people coming here for pancake therapy after dreaded vet appointments.

"Should we get another dog?" Dan asks.

This starts the tears all over again.

"You're not making any sense," says Dan.

"I thought dogs were supposed to teach us how to live," I say.

"Maybe Boomer did," he says.

"He was the perfect guy," I agree.

"Woof, woof," says Dan. "I could try to take his place. Then, "Where would I lick you, anyway?"

I try not to laugh. And then I'm giggling. This makes Dan reach for my hand.

We look at each other. Love syrup floats above our pancakes. We connect.

Dan's beeper goes off. He turns away, mutters several 'uh huhs' then locks my eyes queerly. "The head hunter from Texas. I have to talk to her." He points to the check, then to my handbag, shoulders the phone and waves. He manages to take one last forkful of pancake, and then bolts out of the restaurant. The door slams as Dan dashes to his Caddy. I watch it shoot out to the street, and then how it speeds crazily down Ventura Boulevard.

He calls me from the car. "I told her Texas is out of the question," he says.

"Thank you. Does this have something to do with Boom?"

"I'm not really sure. Maybe." Pause. "Probably. Yeah. Of course!" Long silence. "I guess want to be generous and affable. I want to be loved as much as he was."

Once more time, our dog saves us.

I promise to make Dan pizza from scratch.

Home. For hours, I think I see my dog everywhere. Shadows, movement, flashes of his tender, rheumy brown eyes.

About the Author:

Barbara Bottner has authored over forty-five books for children, some NYTimes Bestsellers, including YA novels. She has written for the LA Weekly, The Miami Herald, reviews for the NYTimes, LATimes Book review, published short stories in COSMOPOLITAN, PLAYGIRL as well as acted with LA Mama in NY and Europe. Her animated shorts won "Best Film For TV" in the Annecy Animation Festival, Other won CINE Golden Eagles. She has had pieces performed by the Jewish Women's Theater and also does Spoken Word in LA

THE DAY THE RICHEST POLE DIED
by Ewa Mazierska

The Rs. lived in the last house on our road, in central, yet rural and god-forsaken Poland. One hundred metres north from them was a statue of the Holy Mary, which marked the end of our village. Furthermore there were fields for two or three kilometres, then a railway line and then another village began. During communist times there was always competition between ours and the other village, because the other village had a railway station, while we had a church. When I was a child, the statue marked for me the end of a familiar, safe world. Beyond there were 'the others': people whom I knew nothing of and who felt like a threat. I saw the Rs. as the guardians of our small world and they adopted such a role, informing the neighbours about the developments on the other side. But they were never gossipy or malicious, perhaps because they were the poorest in the neighbourhood and all their energies were invested in surviving the daily hardship.

The old R., whose Christian name I did not know had a small plot of land behind his house, three hectares or so, and worked as a bricklayer in a construction firm in Włocławek, the closest large town. He thus belonged to the category of peasant-workers, who had low status because for the peasants they were not sufficiently rural, and for the workers they were not working class. But most likely he did not care about his status; maybe he was not even fully aware of it. His wife, Franka, as long as I remember, was working the fields; their own plot of land and those of more affluent farmers. She was known for being very good in this work, particularly harvesting potatoes and onions. She was two to three times faster than an average worker, therefore in summer her service was in high demand. The Rs. lived first in a wooden house, which previously belonged to Franka's parents until R. built a small house from a more durable material, which looked like pieces of concrete blocks, used in the 1970s for building high-rise estates. I guess he lifted them from the construction sites on which he was employed. The house seemed to be unfinished, with more windows planned than built, yet was also covered with scars and had aged prematurely, with walls falling apart before they were fully erected. This was despite the fact that the R. (not unlike another builder on our street, the father of my best friend) was spending every weekend on improving his house. After R.'s death the house became surrounded by extensions. They grew like cancer on, by comparison, a healthy body of the main house, being made of poorer materials, with few, very small, windows. For a reason unknown to me the extended parts were dangerously close to the road, although the owners had plenty of space on the other side. Maybe because of having too few windows or to avoid falling into the ditch, the Rs. kept the doors always open, which allowed the passers-by to (over)hear their conversations. Such a habit was acceptable then, when the right to privacy was curtailed by the state, but after the fall of the old system, when people's class position could be easily guessed from the height of their gates and the length of their fences, people like the Rs. started to be seen as a 'problem' waiting to be solved.

By the time R. had finished the first version of his house, the Rs. had one daughter, Maria, and twin sons, Marek and Maciek. R. died when Franka was pregnant with their fourth child, Basia, who was born about fifteen years after their first child. At primary school I was in the same class as Maria. With her dark-blue, velvety eyes and dark hair, common among Mediterranean women, but exceptionally rare in central Poland, she was the prettiest girl in our year. However, she was a very poor pupil. Barely able to read, write and count, she was always on the verge of being sent off to the class for children with learning disabilities. She has repeated some years and finished her education after primary school. Before she reached twenty, she was married to the son of a local peasant, who was also the most unpleasant character in our class. After her wedding Maria disappeared from my radar and indeed she was no longer seen on our road. When I asked Franka what happened to her daughter she replied that she gave birth to a disabled child who was bed-ridden. Consequently, Maria was also, more or less, bed-ridden, taking full responsibility for caring for her offspring. Franka did not hide the fact that Maria's husband mistreated her daughter, accusing her of producing a substandard child. Franka shed a tear when she mentioned it. It was around this time that Franka started to drink, to calm her heart. What she drank she labelled 'little cherry' (wisienka). It was the common name for cheap, fruity wine, regarded by heavier drinkers as extremely unhealthy, although probably much less so than vodka.

Franka's twin sons disappeared from our village soon after they reached adulthood. One joined the army; the other went to work in a coalmine in the South of Poland. The professional soldier fought in Iraq and Afghanistan, got medals for bravery and eventually settled in the South of Poland. He broke ties with his family, apparently on the request of his wife. For his mother, he was a traitor. The miner returned, although initially he did not move back to the village, only brought his daughter, Vanessa, to be looked after temporarily by her grandma, when he was going through a divorce. The girl stayed with the Rs. for two years. As with her aunt, she was an exceptional beauty, with dark eyes, dark hair, large soft lips and glasses which afforded her an intellectual look. She was also gentle, intelligent and discreet. One could talk with her for hours, but do not learn anything about her family or housing situation. Later I noticed that she was friends with the girls from the best houses, without

searching for their favours. Eventually Vanessa moved with her father to a nearby town and I stopped seeing her. Franka said that she went to university. Apparently she occasionally visited her grandma and kept in touch with her old friends.

Basia was described by the people in our village as the one who 'did not know her father'. First I took it merely as a statement of the fact, resulting from his premature death. But then I realised there was something more to it: Basia did not know the Freudian 'name of the father': patriarchal authority. Maybe because of that, from an early age she was keen on boys, which inevitably led to gossip. I saw Basia as a transitory figure. In many ways she was a child of Eastern European communism. Although apparently smarter than her older sister, she neglected school and saw no value in education. As with Maria, it never occurred to her that she could do something with her life: get a job or a stall in a market. Unlike her older sister, however, who suffered in silence, she wanted something better from life and acquired some bourgeois habits. She changed the colour of her hair, from super-black to strawberry blond, which did not suit her, painted her toenails and confessed to me that she could not get out of bed without drinking two cups of strong coffee. Basia also did not like to get drunk on 'cherry', preferring vodka mixed with Coca-Cola. Moreover, unlike her mother or sister, Basia did not want just to get married. Her greatest dream was to marry the richest man in Poland. This angered her mother, who used to repeat that all rich men are arseholes: they get rich by taking from the poor.

In our village there was no match for Basia. People there did not have much money and for those better off than the Rs., despite her beauty, Basia had little value, which was further lowered by her being 'easy'. To fulfil her dream, she had to look further afar. The man whom she found turned out to be a short, plump man with coarse features, but he exuded an aura of self-confidence, which some people took for charisma. When he stood at the Rs.' courtyard with his legs spread and arms on his hips, he reminded me of Henry VIII from the famous portrait by Hans Holbein. One could assume that the whole estate was his.

Therefore he did not want to work on it; he only requested various changes so that he would not be ashamed to settle there. It did not take Franka much time to figure out that he was a gangster. He turned out to be one of the lowest order. For some years he was robbing provincial shops before being promoted to managing a flock of Romanian prostitutes walking the road near the forest surrounding Włocławek. Whether Basia was aware of that before she tied the knot with him, nobody knew, but most likely it would have made no difference. What counted was that he brought her the luxuries she yearned for: a VHS player, a mobile phone and a car. Well, he did not give her the car, he merely took her for rides and then brought her home. Franka suspected that all these goods were stolen and warned Basia that if their origin was discovered she might get into trouble, but Basia only told her mother to shut up. For her a stolen TV was better than no TV.

Where Basia's husband's permanent address was or even what part of Poland he came from, nobody knew. When asked about his whereabouts, Basia replied that he travelled a lot for business. Later she mentioned that he was building for them a large house near Warsaw, but she was unable to name the suburb where this mansion was to be erected. For the time being, Basia was thus stuck in her old family adobe. Franka alleged that her son in law had a house, but he used it as a training ground for his foreign 'whores'. This situation, in Franka's view, was doubly demeaning for Basia, because she had no access to his house and was below his female employees, who knew more about his life than his family. Franka hated her son in law from the first time she saw him and her loathing grew the more she learnt about him. She never mentioned his name and called him 'This Pimp', 'This Bastard' or 'This Motherfucker', the last name because, as she put it, he was the type who would fuck his own mother if it would bring him profit. She also lost heart for her daughter for being greedy, naïve and a burden to her.

Soon after meeting her future husband, Basia became pregnant and gave birth to a boy, whom she called Bernard. Two years later Brad was born. Such foreign-sounding names, in her

mind, testified to her elevated social status. For Franka they only showed that Basia did not know her place. She polonised them, calling one Benek, and the other Bronek. The older boy was like his father: short and plump and with blondish hair, and he adopted the posture of Henry VIII. The younger had Basia's Mediterranean appearance and came across as soft and shy. The older used to call his mother 'You stupid whore'; the younger cuddled to her and cried when his brother insulted her.

The father brought his sons computer games and flashy clothes and took them for rides in his car, in the same way he did earlier with their mother. After performing this ritual he disappeared, to return after weeks or months in increasingly battered vehicles, with some flashy gadgets which, after some time, stopped impressing his sons, as their school mates pointed to their cheapness and obsolescence. The stream of gadgets stopped when he went to prison. Franka hoped that it would put an end to her daughter's ungraceful liaison, but she was proved wrong. Basia remained loyal to her husband and kept visiting him every month or so, as often really as she could afford, given that he lived now over two hundred kilometres from her. She even occasionally engaged in remunerative activity, such as child minding or cleaning, to afford train tickets and presents for her man, so that she did not feel inferior to the wives of other prisoners. Basia got no support from her husband's gangster pals, proving to Franka that not only was he scum, but the lowest sort, commanding no respect even from his own ilk. Franka got so exasperated by the situation that she started to smoke, which, by her own account, burned her lungs and made her weak. Still, despite now being in her seventies, she worked the fields as before because paying for the basics such as food and electricity, was more difficult than ever. As if the situation was not bad enough, during the year of heavy rains their house was flooded. Water destroyed the floors, the meagre furniture and most of the luxuries Basia got from her husband. A neighbour visiting them after this tragedy saw a Nintendo Playstation floating in a pool of dirty water, as if it was a ship. They got no insurance money as their house was, obviously, not insured. Moreover, the flooding revealed that the damaged extensions were built without permission. Franka got a letter asking her to demolish their remains and pay a hefty fine, but it was waived by the local council clerk, proving that people are not heartless or that Polish clerks still enjoy some autonomy. Thanks to the pressure from the neighbours they also got some financial help from the council to repair their house and one neighbour arranged a collection of money and other goods to give to Franka. Normally we would not do it, knowing that she would refuse any help, but this accumulation of misfortune stripped her of some of her pride and she accepted. It also stripped her of her faith in God. 'God died with communism or he is as much of a motherfucker as my son in law,' she said.

After the flooding social services got interested in the welfare of Basia's sons, which added to Franka's stress. Despite loathing her daughter and her son in law, she did not want to lose the boys. Around this time Basia got pregnant again. Her third child was conceived in prison, shortly after the authorities introduced conjugal visits. Nine months after such a visit Basia's youngest son was born. For Franka it was a sign of hope. She loved the boy more than Bernard and Brad because 'he did not know his father.' She herself chose a name for him, Jan, which turned out to be the name of her late husband. However, the new child made things even more difficult than before. Almost every week now Franka and Basia received visits from high-heeled women, who smirked at their poverty and the alleged low standard of hygiene, and warned them that if they did not prove themselves worthy of their children, they would lose them. Franka recounted the visits with the highest indignation. If not for the children, she would have punched these women, who she perceived as getting money from the state which they should have been receiving. Basia was less worried about these visits, having other issues on her mind. These were to do with her husband. While before he kept his family away from his criminal operations, now, being constrained, he wanted her to act as his proxy. What exactly Basia did for him, nobody knew, but her activities upset some people. It was proven one night when two men with their faces covered entered their house and shot

Jan. He died on the spot. Why the baby was targeted, rather than Basia or her older sons? The answers to these questions were sought by the neighbours in the months to come. The prevailing hypothesis was that his death had a symbolic value – it was a sign to Basia to stay away from the turf wars in which her husband was engaged.

The murder of Basia's son took place the same day the richest Pole died, in a hospital in Vienna, where he was undergoing some revolutionary treatment, which, however, failed. Judging by its reporting in the news, a saint had passed away. His right to sainthood was ensured by his wealth and his philanthropy. The unspoken assumption of almost everybody publicly commemorating his life, including some high-ranking priests, was that the more wealth, the more charity. For some people in our village the death of the Polish tycoon was, on the other hand, some consolation – a proof that little Jan was somewhat equal to the wealthiest of the world. But others drew attention to their difference: one violent and committed in a household lacking basic amenities; the other in a comfortable and hygienic environment, in a foreign location, underlining the billionaire's cosmopolitan outlook; one happening before conscious life properly started; the other when the man had achieved practically everything there was to achieve and had reached retirement age. For them it was a sign there was no justice in death as there was no justice in life. But the effect of the coincidence of these two deaths was that the demise of the rich man made the neighbours remember the day the boy died. After that whenever anyone asked when little Jan died, the answer was that 'it was the day the richest Pole died.'

In the next three months or so the house of Rs. was emptied. Basia was taken to stand trial for abetting her husband's crimes. Bernard and Brad were sent to foster families. Franka suffered a stroke and was taken to the hospital, where she died without regaining consciousness. The house and the farm were put up for sale and several months later bought by the richest farmer in the neighbouring village. He demolished the Rs' shack and built there a two-storey house for his daughter. Unlike the Rs.'

house, which was almost touching the road and revealed its guts to everybody who wanted to look at it, this one was built at a large distance from the road and was best protected of all the houses on our street, with a high fence and three dogs guarding it. Some neighbours showed the house to their visitors saying with bitterness: 'this is our future.'

About the Author:

Ewa Mazierska is a historian of film and popular music, working at the University of Central Lancashire. She writes short stories in her spare time. Her stories were published in several literary magazines and shortlisted in competitions.

FLICKERS OF LIGHT

by Hina Ahmed

"Our deepest fear is not that we are inadequate. Our deepest fear is that we are powerful beyond measure. It is our light not our darkness that most frightens us." --MaryAnne Williamson

April 2014: School

"Where is the boy Ms. Zareena Khan?" Where is he? The principal of the school asked her like the badgering of a woodpecker on a dead tree. Zareena stood looking before the parking lot, bustling and alive with children, but Zayan was nowhere to be seen.

How could she? How could she lose a child?

October 2015: Zareena's bedroom

"I just wanted to let you know that I delivered a healthy baby boy last night!" The text message flashed on Zareena's cell phone screen.

"That is great! I am very happy for you!" Zareena exclaimed, relieved that text messages were able to hide the yearnings of the heart.

September 2016: School

"You have been assigned to work with a special needs second grade boy named Michael. This is temporary matter until we find a full-time placement," the secretary stated as Zareena entered the main office of the school.

All eyes were on her as she made her way into what reminded her of the cold, fluorescently lighted chambers of an international airport, with its wide hallways, and grandiose, hanging displays of art. She walked with her austere, marble colored glasses and sharp new hair cut that accentuated the delicacy of her jaw line, and the fragility of the femininity of her features, marked by the subtle, silver gem that rested on the left side of her nose; a sculpted face, made by none other than the conscientious hands of her generous Creator; the modesty of her beauty served to magnify it in all the ways that invoked the green laced envy that grew like tangled vines on chalked faces that Zareena sought to briskly walk past on her way to the classroom.

"Hi Michael!" Zareena exclaimed upon first meeting him. "Hello," he responded jovially, wearing a t-shirt of giant cheeseburgers and flying spaghetti monsters, with his protruding little belly, and short, spiky strands of blonde hair that rested on the top of his head like a freshly mowed lawn. Michael: the epitome of a lovable, huggable boy, with his perfectly round face that glistened like snow in the dark, and eyes that radiated with the dancing charm of both the curiosity and mischief of an unyielding youth. Michael: The perfect American boy.

"Make sure he takes walking breaks every thirty minutes, and make sure that he goes to the bathroom exactly when he needs to, or he gets restless, and he has to sit in his wooden chair while on the floor, or he just won't pay attention...and he also needs gum, at several intervals throughout the day..." the lead classroom teacher instructed frantically as 'orders from his mother,' as she ran from one end of the classroom to the other in last minute preparations for the first day of school.

Things started to take shape within the first week of student acclimation.

"You can't be giving that much attention to Dayshawn. He is way behind grade-level. Don't waste your time with him. You need to stick with Michael," the lead teacher prompted.

September 2016: Zareena's home

"Let's make America great again!" Roared a voice over the evening television screen, as Zareena's father Omar looked on with the alertness that is invoked from an internal disturbance. Omar scoffed at the implications of the man's remarks, as Zareena viewed the television screen with her father in a state of equal condemnation. "You know the majority of doctors in the hospital we work in were not even born in this country. Does this man not realize the contribution of immigrants?" Zareena's brother Abdulla said as he profusely chewed on the taut marrow of his chicken bone.

"Well, I can say that after being in this country for over thirty years, we will at best be second class citizens," Omar said resting his face in his hands, as he continued to look on the television screen with eyes filled with the sorrow of migration.

Back in School

"I am sorry, but we cannot have you filling in for the one-to-one position with Michael anymore. We are looking for someone full-time. However, we do need substitute teachers for our other positions." The school secretary said to Zareena on her way out of the school.

Zareena spent the remainder of the next two weeks filling in for other grade levels where she was needed, but she found herself lost in thoughts of working with Michael: the eccentric, lovable, huggable boy.

"Ugh. The new woman who got hired to work with Michael is awful, just awful, I want you back!" The lead teacher said to Zareena in a state of flurry while passing her in the hallway one afternoon.

"Oh, really?"

"Yes! Tomorrow morning, you and I will go talk to the principal, and I will get you back!" She said before scurrying down the hallway.

The following morning Zareena and the lead teacher approached the principal.

"Zareena would like to come back and work with Michael, you know she was just so good with him and I would really love to have her back," the lead teacher said in a state of desperation. Zareena stood silently beside her with a look of passive compliance.

"If Zareena goes to the district office and changes her position from a substitute teacher to that of a 1:1 teacher we will be able to hire her for the position," the principal remarked curtly.

The District's Office

"Are you sure? Are you sure you want to resign as a substitute teacher? You realize the significant pay cut, as well as the status shift that will come from switching your position?" The administrator said to Zareena in shock with her request.

"Yes. I realize that, but I think I have really grown attached to this child. He needs me." Zareena said.

"Well, alright, if that is your decision. I will go get the appropriate paperwork," the administrator stated.

December 2016

For as much as Zareena loved Michael, her love, like all love was tested. Especially when it came to having him complete his writing tasks.

"If you don't stop Michael, I will have to tell your mother," Zareena said, as he refused to do the writing prompt.

"No!" Michael squealed as he abruptly got up, ran around her, took his hand and struck it forcefully over her mouth.

"Silence!" He screamed.

January 20, 2017

"Silence Class!"

We are going to spend the rest of the day watching the inauguration of our new President, the lead teacher announced in a state of euphoria, as Zareena looked on with all due respect.

June 2017

"You know, you have done such a wonderful job working with Michael. The family needs a care provider to work with him at their home over the summer. You would be great for the job," The occupational therapist said to Zareena during the last week of school. Zareena paused.

"You know, you don't have to take the position, but maybe think about it." She added before leaving the room.

Zareena had no serious plans over the summer. She wanted it to be that way. This job with Michael would give her a little spending money and seemed like it would be easy enough.

The following week Zareena announced: "Well...I decided. I will take the job!"

July 2017: Michael's home

Zareena approached the house on the brink of the hill. It was a one story home made of bricks, resting on a small yard, with barren soil and a broken driveway, deteriorating with rumbling rocks, where a worn down, rusted mini van sat slumped and exhausted from the weight of carrying a heavy burden. Zareena rang the doorbell.

"Come in, the door is open!" Hollered the voice of a woman. Zareena entered the home that smelled of both children and their pets on hot summer days. The blinds were shut, the windows closed. A dark dankness penetrated through creaking cracks in the hard, wooden floors that were covered in boxes upon boxes of material goods of dire need.

Michael's mother, Diane sat at the head of a wooden table, her blonde hair thrown up carelessly, her face plain and unadorned, with the potential for a country like beauty of simplicity, but one that had lost itself.

"Oh, don't worry about taking off your shoes, we are not like those people," she said as Zareena stopped herself from doing what had been her childhood habit upon entering a home.

"So, basically, my son has thousands of dollars in his budget in terms of the services he can receive with his disability," Diane proclaimed.

"Oh, wow, that must have been a difficult process to receive," Zareena stated.

"Yes, you have no idea, but I did it," Diane responded.

"You know what would be great for you to watch in order to get some context into working with Michael? Watch the film 'Gifted,' it sums up my son very well," Diane said proudly.

Zareena was intrigued by the endless assortment of magnetic monkeys on Diane's refrigerator. In one particular image Diane held the face of a gorilla next to hers, her eyes closed, her face softened by the tranquility that comes from sharing tender affection.

"Wow, you seem to be so fond of them," Zareena said touched by the photo.

"I am. You know they are easy to love once they have been trained to do what you need them to do," Diane replied.

Summer Days

Zareena's summer days were spent taking Michael around town, playing in the parks, taking him swimming, and going to the museums: the perfect summer job indeed.

"Come on Ms. K! Come into the water with me!" Michael screamed from the lake, as he splashed around like a fearless, flapping fish.

Zareena tepidly walked to the edge of the lake in her bathing suit, feeling the penetrating eyes of the large bystanders on her small body, hearing their jarring voices in her head:

Perhaps that is her adopted son...he is far too white to be her actual son...then again anything is possible these days...is this woman even permitted to be with this child? Faces compounded by both confusion and suspicion left Zareena with both inner sensations of pulsating pleasures and disorienting disturbances.

"Come on Ms. K! Be the unicorn that I wish to ride!" Michael requested as Zareena got into the water next to him and Michael climbed onto her back, as she took him for a swim: the magical, swimming, unicorn, and her heroic rider.

August 2017

"It is so great that Michael has you, that you love him so much, thank you so much for all that you do, I really don't know what we would do without you," a text message from Diane appeared before her.

It is nice to be needed. To be wanted. Zareena thought.

In a home, outside of home:

"Michael really wants to meet our family cat, Misty, is it ok to bring him to my home?" Zareena asked Diane via text message.

"Sure," she replied.

"Ok, now before entering you need to make sure to take off your shoes and I don't want you running around like crazy got it?" Zareena said more sternly than her usual self as they arrived on the driveway of her home.

"Ummi! I have a special visitor!" Zareena hollered to her mother; her voice echoing through the large foyer as they stepped on shiny, white, floors made of untarnished marble.

"Oh…what a surprise…hello…" Ayesha said, in her trying to be welcoming voice, as she made her way down the stairs, as Michael looked around like a domestic cat brought into the wilderness for the first time.

"It is nice to meet you Michael," Ayesha said shaking his hand. Michael, suddenly coy, looked down and smiled innocently.

Zareena took his hand and led him to the living room, sitting next to him. Ayesha sat on the opposite side of them, looking on.

"So, what do you like to do Michael?" Ayesha asked, attempting to make conversation with the boy that had won over the heart of her daughter.

Michael: restless, eager to move. "Michael, Mrs. K asked you a question, what do you like to do?" Zareena reiterated, looking at him intently, as Ayesha's face suddenly fell to clouds of sadness.

Michael made his way over to the mosque monument that rested on the table in the foyer and turned it on.

"Allah Akabar!" The monument rang loudly.

"Ah!" What is that? Michael said as he jumped. "That is our call to prayer, as Muslims."

Ayesha suddenly interjected enthusiastically. "You know, Islam is a religion that…." But Michael was already half way through the family room, where he found the cat.

"Here Michael, hold my hand and I will give you a tour of our house." Zareena said leading him into the kitchen.

"Ah! What is that smell?" He asked in frightful awe. "That is my mom's Pakistani curry, remember I told you that we were from Pakistan?"

"See." Zareena said as she lifted the cover to the dish, the hot steam invigorating Michael's face, as he gazed in, and then abruptly made his way to the fruit pile and helped himself to the sweet, decadence of a juicy plum, digging his mighty teeth into its bursting flavor, "this is delicious!" he proclaimed in a state of exhilarated intoxication, the plum's purple residue smearing the perfection of his skin, as he continued to make his way through the rest of the house; Zareena following like a sheep behind him.

"I met Michael today, he came to our ghar," Ayesha revealed to her husband Omar that evening. "Oh. He came to the house?" Omar asked, suddenly unable to sip his tea.

Exchanges At the Kitchen Table

"You know, since you work with my other children, just add some extra hours so that you can get paid more, I don't want you to think that this job is not worth it for you." Diane said.

"Oh, ha. I don't mind playing with them, making up hours would probably be just a little bit unethical!" Zareena said with a hint of sarcasm.

"Unethical? No. I don't think so. Just do it," Diane remarked.

"You want to teach children in the inner city? Do you understand that they will most likely rape you? You will not make it out alive. You are really great with children, but you need to be working with children like Michael, not those kids that will just end up working in Burger King. Don't waste your time." Diane said looking Zareena in the eye.

"Did that woman in the water not understand to evacuate the city? What is wrong with these people?" Diane retorted in response to the images of the Houston flooding on the news.

"So what is your plan?" Diane asked.

"My plan? Like my life plan?" Zareena laughed.

"No silly. Your plan with Michael, what's your plan with my son?" Diane asked.

"Oh come here Michael let me fold your jeans up so that you can put your rain boots on properly," Zareena said, as she kneeled down in front of him.

"Oh, stop Ms. K! You are just crazy! Let me show you the way this is done." Diane interjected.

"You know, you don't have to call me Ms. K, you can call me Zareena."

"No. Ms. K... it just suits you so well," Diane responded.

"Ms. K, my daughter Mallory's birthday is coming up. I will email you an image of the gift that she would just love to have. Ofcourse, don't feel obligated to buy it or anything."

"I really think you will end up marrying a white man, tell your family to stop trying to pair you up with a South Asian man!" Diane declared one evening. "In fact, let me message my one cousin, he is amazing. He would be the perfect husband for you."

Meanwhile, Michael's younger sister:

Mallory screamed in anger

Running to the refuge of

Zareena's safe arms

Wanting to hide in them

Forever

From the scorching flames

Of the inflaming voice of her mother

"Ms. K cannot save you!"

Her mother roared

Screaming in terror

The child fled to the chambers

Of her fortified room

The glorified Nanny, with a master's degree,

The brown Savior

Of white mothers and their children

Sit.

Empty handed in the homes of their Oppressors

"Zareena, you need to understand what this woman is doing. She is using her power over you, to guilt you into staying in this job, that quite frankly you seem to not even want!" Zareena's friend Zion stated to her over coffee.

Zareena looked on at him with the pouty sullenness that comes from hearing the hard truth. "Yes. You are right. I don't even want this job. Yet, here I am. Feeling stuck, feeling like this woman's children are mine, saturated, completely...by feelings of a despairing guilt!" Zareena exclaimed in devastated self-realization, sitting haplessly before him.

"Break free Zareena, break free from the chains of the oppressor."

"But, Zion, for all the ways in which you are right, I cannot help but see the humanness in her. In me. In us both."

In those moments of your

Helpless defeat,

Of your angry anguish

Of your sullen eyes filled with a dooming despair

Of longings for a life that could be

Something other than what it is

I see in the emptiness of your watered gaze,

A reflection I cannot run from.

October 2017: Laps of Affection, Words of Hate

One evening Diane's youngest daughter Katie decided to crawl up into her lap like a cat; Zareena more than willing to rub her back with affection.

"You like Ms. K that much, huh? Diane said staring at her daughter with piercing eyes. Why don't you go and live with her and her mOzlem family? She said, like the sudden hiss of a venomous snake.

That evening, Zareena stopped and parked her car in front of her favorite soothing tree, staring at it for what seemed to be hours, unable to stop thinking about Diane's words.

Her and her Mozlem family.

Words sitting like cemented, wet spit on her face.

How could she? Why would she? As much as Zareena wanted to pretend it did not happen, she could not get her words out of her mind. But more importantly, Zareena had no choice but to confront the unveiled ideology behind them; the haunting secrets of Diane's heart overtly emerged, engulfing her into the darkness of her heart's inner most chambers.

But then, there were the children.

The children who had her heart.

The children that found refuge in her lap.

The children who loved her love.

But, the love that loves, also chains one's feet to the ground.

"She is not my mother!" Michael's words of the past shook her.

"But they are not your children!" Zion's words reminded her.

In Bed Wide Awake

The image of Michael's baby sister, Adele flashed before Zareena's eyes as she lay in bed wide awake that night.

The tender, soft feet

Delicate and fragile

Healing the broken, bruised hands

Of the people doing their bidding

Grow up to become

The thudding thuds

Of loud feet in combat boots

Ready for battle.

Voices of the past came suddenly flooding through her:

"Zareena. I want you hear now. Right now, right this instant, get in the car and just drive, just drive to me," Christopher commanded over the phone in the voice of utmost urgency.

"I just want to dig in, dig it into your sweetness, and taste it, taste it on the tips of my tongue."

After the ordeal, Zareena perused through her facebook page as a numbing ritual, as Christopher planted himself directly in front of her face and demanded her to:

Gag herself.

Zareena felt Michael's hands fearlessly placed on her mouth as if they had the right to be there:

"Silence!" The memories flooded through her like a devastating tsunami.

October 13, 2017

"I Quit."

Zareena stated via text message to Diane. And then, she quickly clicked:

Block.

"You need to call Diane. She is very upset," read Diane's husband's text message.

Zareena quickly clicked:

Block.

Freedom is never earned through the asking of permission.

Zareena parked her car, as it sat still under the bright sun. She got out of the driver's seat and climbed over to the passenger side of the vehicle. She took her favorite handmade crochet blanket infused with the rich hues of blue, purple, and red, and placed it over her delicate body. She closed her eyes. Yet, even amidst the darkness that ensued, she could still see the faint flickering of light.

About the Author:

Hina Ahmed is a writer from Binghamton, New York. She holds a BA in history and an MA in education from Binghamton University. She enjoys writing poetry, short stories, political essays, and is in the midst of a forthcoming novel: The Dance of the Firefly. She has had her work published in NYU's Aftab Literary Magazine, East Lit Journal, Archer Magazine, Pipe Dream, Press and Sun Bulletin, among others. When she is not writing, she is probably talking about how she should be writing.

THE CHOICE

by Zia Marshall

Kaira stood at the edge of the water, watching the frothy waves as they swept over her bare feet before receding into the distant ocean. The waves danced over her feet, sometimes vigorously and at other times in a smooth almost silky motion. How eternal the ocean was, Kaira thought, as she stared at it for a long peaceful moment fixing the image in her artist's eye. Day changed into night, the seasons slipped by, but the ocean remained the same, its waves eternally roiling with froth and bubble as they lapped against the shores before receding into the distant blue and then returning once again.

Kaira walked back to her cottage, which was just a short distance from the shore. She had been lucky to find this house, she thought, as she slid the key into the door and entered. Most of the sea-facing properties had long been snapped up in the sleepy, seaside town of Kollam. But its owner, old Mrs. D'souza, who had recently lost her husband, had put up this house for sale. She had wanted to move to Mumbai so that she could be close to her children. Kaira had just arrived in town and heard the house was for sale. She had immediately made an offer – that was a little more than the asking price just to make sure Mrs. D'souza wasn't tempted by a better offer. That had been almost a year ago and Kaira had happily settled into the little cottage.

It was a good life, she reflected, as she walked into the kitchen to fix her usual breakfast – a mug of coffee and toast with some marmalade smeared over it. Then setting the coffee and toast on a tray, she made her way to the dining table where she had an uninterrupted view of the ocean from the large picture window. She sipped her coffee as she watched the sea glittering in the early morning light like a thousand tiny diamonds were strewn over its surface.

Joe walked into the room just then. "Mooning over the ocean again," Joe teased, slipping into a chair and grabbing a toast from Kaira's plate. "I don't get it, you know. Most people tire of the ocean after a couple of months. It becomes part of the regular scenery. But you are something else, Kaira! You stare at it every single day as if you are seeing it for the very first time."

Kaira turned to look at Joe with a sheepish grin. "I know Joe, most people find it odd. But I can't help it, honestly I can't. I feel very drawn to the sea – it calls to my soul..."

"Oh God! It's too early in the morning for your artist-shartist philosophy Kair, drop it please," Joe complained, grabbing the coffee mug from Kaira's hand and taking a long sip of coffee.

"Oh I needed that. Here you can finish the rest, I don't mind," Joe said, setting down the cup before Kaira and grinning impishly at her.

"Thanks," Kaira grinned back. "My morning coffee would taste odd if you didn't steal a couple of sips from it. But why won't you fix yourself a cup? Or shall I do it for you?"

"No time, sweetie. Got to run. Rahul will be in office by ten and I need to run these plans by him before the client meeting at twelve and then...."

"Carry on, Joe" Kaira said. "I'll finish up here and head for the studio. Will you be in for lunch?"

"Not sure," Joe called, grabbing the keys from the foyer table and dashing out of the house.

Kaira's mobile rang just then. Frowning, she glanced down to see who was calling. It was her mother. Briefly she contemplated ignoring the call. Then shrugging, she decided to get it over with.

"Hello, Mum!"

"Hi sweetie, you haven't called in so long. I was worried!"

"We spoke two days ago, Mum," Kaira said struggling to contain her impatience.

"Well, did you think about what we discussed last time?"

"About moving back to Mumbai? Honestly, Mum why would I do that? I am happy here. This place is so beautiful and I am finally able to paint. I am selling my paintings and making a decent living. I have a great set of friends. Why on earth would I give all this up and move back to a crowded city?"

"But you can paint anywhere, can't you darling? It's not like you have a real office job or anything to keep you in Kollum."

Kaira sighed. "I couldn't paint in Mumbai, remember? I just couldn't...I felt like the city was stifling me. Here I feel like I have finally found my muse..."

"Oh Kaira, don't start all that arty talk with me, darling. It's not like painting is a real job or what you will be doing for the rest of your life. Eventually you will have to grow up, get a regular job and settle down into a career. You were so intent on painting that Dad and I thought you should give it a go. But it can't last forever, can it?"

"I don't see why not!" Kaira burst out angrily. "My paintings are selling well and I am making decent money. Why do I feel I have to justify my life and what I do every single time I speak with you? It's so annoying! Just because I don't have a career and a nine-to-five office job, it doesn't mean I don't work hard, Mum! Because I do! I am an artist! Just accept me for who I am please."

"All right Kaira! There's really no need to get so upset. Now before I forget … the real reason why I rang up is Anita Shankar came to visit me the other day. There's a boy she'd like you to meet..."

"Mum, stop! I am not meeting any boys! And that's final. I thought I made that clear the last time we spoke on this subject."

"Yes, but this is such a good match, Kaira. Why don't you just meet him? There's no harm in it, is there?"

"No! Not happening!"

"But Kaira, you are twenty-three darling. Isn't it time you started thinking of settling down?"

"Ma, I've got to go! There's someone at the door. I'll talk to you later..."

Kaira set down her mobile with a guilty sigh. She loved her mother but honestly they just weren't on the same wavelength. Her mother didn't understand the life she had chosen to lead. She was eternally struggling to make her fit into the conventional mold but Kaira was just not made that way! Why couldn't her mother understand?

The conversation had upset her more than she realized and she walked into the kitchen to fix herself a cup of coffee. Then with the mug in her hand she made herself calm down. If not the day would be a disaster and she would never be able to paint. And she needed to finish Lavanya's orders. Lavanya wanted a set of six paintings for her new home – it was a large order and Kaira needed to finish it by the end of the month.

A few hours later, Kaira was humming to herself as she worked in her studio. She added the finishing touches to the third painting in the set and stepped back with a sigh of satisfaction to survey her work. Yes! It was good even if she said so herself. Lavanya was sure to like it. And since he had such a wide social circle, Kaira was hoping that she would bag other orders when Lavanya's friends saw her paintings.

Glancing at her watch, Kaira realized it was six in the evening. The hours had flown by and she hadn't realized the time. Walking into the kitchen, she hurriedly started fixing dinner. Joe, who was eternally hungry, would be home any minute. Kaira smiled to herself as she thought of Joe! Who would have thought that she could have found someone who would become so special in such a short space of time? So what if it wasn't the most conventional of relationships – she cared a hoot about all that! All she cared about was that Joe brought out the best in her. She was a different person thanks to Joe. It was Joe who had encouraged her to reach out for her dreams and try her hand at painting. If it hadn't been for Joe, she would never have had the courage to do so.

"I'm home," Joe's voice cut across her thoughts. She glanced down and realized that she hadn't even started on dinner. Joe walked into the kitchen and smiled.

"Did the artist lose track of time again?" Joe asked. "Here let me take over." Soon Joe had things under control. There was a pot of vegetable stew simmering over the flame and some fish fillets in the grill.

"Thanks, Joe," Kaira sighed. I don't know what I would do without you.

"Well, you'd starve for starters," Joe replied, smiling indolently. "Come here, babe? How was your day?"

"It started out with a call from Mum. That didn't go very well. She wants me to meet some boy, but I fobbed her off."

"When are you going to tell her about us, Kai?" Joe asked, glancing down at her quizzically.

"I don't know if I can. And why should I? Can't we just carry on the way we are? Why does anyone need to know about us?"

"Because it's more honest! With your parents, it is also the right thing to do. We can't hide forever, Kaira! People are bound to find out about us sooner or later. Are you ashamed of me, of who I am?"

"No, Joe! Never! But I honestly feel that our relationship is our business. Why do we have to bring other people into it?"

"Because we can't live like this forever, Kaira! Pretending in public that we are just good friends – how long can that carry on? I mean

even our friends are bound to figure things out sooner or later, aren't they? I'm asking again – are you ashamed of who I am? Because if you are, then we should stop right now! Before I start to care too much."

"No, Joe," Kaira wailed. "Don't say that! And don't talk of leaving please. I couldn't bear it if you were no longer a part of my life. But I don't want to share you with others just yet. Can we keep things secret a little longer please? Perhaps in a month or two we can start telling our friends. As for my parents, I am not sure…let's see shall we?"

"Ok!" Joe acquiesced, giving in to Kaira's plea because it was so hard to refuse her anything.

"Let's go for a walk after dinner, shall we?"

Later that night, Kaira tossed and turned restlessly in bed. She mulled over her relationship with Joe. She loved Joe dearly and she knew Joe felt the same about her. But Kaira wasn't sure she could deal with the relationship if it came out into the open. Deep down inside, she knew that while she couldn't imagine life without Joe, she also couldn't deal with the kickback if their relationship came out into the open. Was she ashamed of Joe? She wasn't sure – although she denied it, perhaps she was. She shuddered when she thought of the comments that would follow if people knew that she and Joe were a couple – that they loved each other. How would people react if they knew the reality about Joe? But wasn't Joe's reality, her reality as well? Often Kaira had thought of leaving, of walking away before she became too emotionally entangled in the relationship. But she just couldn't bring herself to do so. She knew she was being a coward, Kaira thought. She loved Joe, but she wasn't ready to commit to the relationship. She wondered if she ever would be! And was she being fair to Joe to keep things in limbo? The questions tossed around in her mind as she drifted off into a restless sleep.

The next morning, when Kaira woke up, Joe had already left for the day. There was an early morning meeting, she supposed as she tossed aside the duvet and walked to the window to throw it open. Pale sunbeams filtered in through the lacy white curtains that were fluttering lazily in the gentle early morning breeze. Kaira showered and walked into the kitchen to fix herself a cup of coffee. The doorbell rang just then.

Who could be calling so early in the morning, Kaira wondered. Opening the door she found herself face to face with her mother.

"Surprise, darling!" Tara Sharma exclaimed.

Kaira stared at her too shocked to take in what she was seeing. "What….what are you doing here, Mum?" she asked.

"Well you won't visit us so I thought I would come down instead and surprise you. What's wrong? You look so shocked!"

"No, it's nothing," Kaira said shaking her head. "I'm just surprised to see you. And happy of course," she added, with a bright smile. Thank god Joe had left early, Kaira thought. She would have to phone and warn Joe not to return home and stay elsewhere for a few days till her mother left. "How long are you planning on staying, Mum?" Kaira asked.

"For a week at least, Kaira or may be two. I'm not sure," her mother replied.

Kaira's mind was in turmoil. A week or two! Where would Joe stay for so long? And worse still what would Joe think? What if her mother's visit brought matters to a head and Joe insisted on coming out into the open. What would she do?

The door opened just then and Joe walked into the room. "Kaira, darling I forgot my laptop in the mad rush this morning…."

"Hello!" Mrs. Sharma exclaimed brightly. "Are you Kaira's friend? I'm her mother, Mrs. Sharma. It's so nice to finally see where Kaira is living and meet her friends. Do you live here as well?"

Joe stared at Kaira's mother in shocked surprise.

Kaira stepped in, desperate to salvage the situation. "Mum this is Joe - a very good friend who is staying with me for a few days."

"Nice to meet you, Joe," Mrs. Sharma said, smiling brightly at the two young people who stood before her. "But isn't Joe an odd name for a girl?"

"Kaira didn't tell you my full name Mrs. Sharma. It's Jyotsna, but my friends call me Joe. Actually there's a lot Kaira hasn't told you. Would you like to do it, Kair? Or shall I?" Joe asked.

Kaira's eyes filled with tears and she shook her head. "Please don't, Joe," she begged.

But Joe was relentless. She had had enough. "Why not, Kair? You have to make a choice. Isn't that what life is all about? Choices? So here's the choice you have to make – are you willing to stand up for who you are? If not, I think it's best if you return home with your mother. Because clearly this life isn't meant for you."

Kaira stared at Joe for a long moment. Why was she pushing her against the wall? Forcing her to choose? And yet Joe had been so clever about it. She hadn't given anything away. Kaira could still leave with her mother, right this moment and no one would know anything about her and Joe. She could choose the conventional path, marriage, children, a real family, all the things her parents wanted for her. Or she could stay here with Joe as her life partner and be prepared to face the consequences of the choice she was making.

"What's happening?" Mrs. Sharma asked in bewilderment, staring at the two girls before her. "What does Kaira need to tell me?"

Joe looked at Kaira. And Kaira stared at her lover as if she were seeing her for very first time. She took in Joe's tumbling, unruly mane of hair that refused to be tamed, her slim figure dressed in what she jokingly referred to as her "office uniform" - a pencil skirt, a formal shirt teamed with a jacket. Joe lit up any room with her very presence. People were drawn to her like bees to honey. And she collected people the way other people collected objects. She had a wide assortment friends and thrived on spending time with them. Her innate honesty had made it hard for her to accept the secrecy that Kaira had insisted on. But she had gone along with it to please her. They hadn't planned on becoming lovers. But it had happened. Friendship had blossomed into love – a love that was rare and sweet and exquisite in the bitter-sweet ecstasy it brought them. Often they found themselves reading each other's thoughts. Each intuitively knew what the other needed and gave it willingly almost unthinkingly.

Had Joe guessed that she wanted her freedom, Kaira wondered. Did Joe know that she sometimes wished she could walk away from the relationship, unscathed, without anyone finding out about it? Was Joe offering her a chance to do this?

"So what will it be, Kaira?" Joe asked.

"Why do I have to decide or choose?" Kaira burst out angrily. "Why can't things carry on as usual? There's nothing wrong in that, is there?"

Joe shook her head stubbornly. "Stop being a child, Kair. You know it can't. So what will it be?"

"I don't know," Kaira replied, miserably.

"I think you should leave, Kair," Joe said gently. "Leave with your Mum. Marry this boy she has chosen. Have children and a real family. Deep down inside, I think that's what you really want."

"Who are you to make up my mind for me," Kaira burst out angrily.

Mrs. Sharma stared at the two girls. She was baffled and couldn't for the life of her understand what was going on. They seemed to be speaking a different language altogether.

"Are you also an artist, Jyotsna?" she asked brightly. "You don't look like one but all this talk sounds very philosophical to me. But thanks for making Kaira see sense. All this painting business is not good for her. She needs a good husband and some children. Then she won't be so restless and unsettled. Go pack your bags, Kaira."

Nodding, Kaira glared at Joe and walked out of the room. Marching into her bedroom, she pulled down the suitcase from the top of the cupboard. Slamming it down on to the bed, she opened the cupboard and furiously started throwing her clothes into the bag. Damn Joe for making her do this, she thought. Tears filled her eyes as she contemplated life without Joe. The thought was almost unbearable. And yet the thought of openly announcing that she was in a relationship with Joe filled her with horror. How would her parents react? And her friends? She couldn't bear the stigma...she just couldn't. The sniggers and the whispers behind her back – they would be like tiny poisoned arrows that would shatter her peace of mind. She doubted she could ever be happy with Joe, once the relationship was out in the open. Damn Joe! They had been so happy, cocooned in their little world and pretending to the outside world that they were two girls sharing a home. Why did people need to know anyway, Kaira thought angrily, as the tears coursed down her cheeks. It was nobody's business, except hers and Joe's. Yet a tiny part of Kaira realized she was fooling herself. Joe was right! They had to make a stand and come out into the open, if they wanted to continue in their relationship. But Kaira lacked the courage to take that stand. Snapping the suitcase shut, she heaved it off the bed. Turning, she glanced briefly at the room where she and Joe had spent so many happy moments. Fleetingly she thought of going into the living room and confessing to her mother. Then her courage failed her. Dragging the suitcase behind her, Kaira walked out of the house, her mother following in bewilderment, wondering why her daughter looked so upset and why she wouldn't even say goodbye to Joe.

Joe stood with her arms folded across her chest watching Kaira leave. There was a flinty look in her eyes. It was for the best, she told herself. Kaira wasn't cut out for this life. She was too vulnerable, too fragile. She cared too much about what people thought of her. It would never have worked if things had come out into the open. Kaira just wasn't tough enough to face the consequences. The whispers and sly innuendoes would have destroyed her and slowly it would have destroyed them as a couple. Better this way, Joe thought. At least she had some precious memories to cling to. They would have to do. Blinking back the tears that threatened to fall, Joe grabbed her laptop and left for work.

Two months later

"Kaira! Here's your soup. Have it while it's still hot," Mrs. Sharma said, as she marched into the room with a steaming bowl of tomato soup.

Kaira was standing at the window staring outside at the bustling traffic on the street far below. She shook her head. "I don't want it, Ma!"

"Kaira, you have to eat, child. Look at you! You have become all skin and bones in just two months. You won't eat, you have stopped painting, and you won't look for a job. All you do is stay in your room, reading and listening to music. What's come over you?"

"Leave me alone, Ma" Kaira said.

Shaking her head, Mrs. Sharma set down the soup and left the room. She would have a word with Dev, she decided. Perhaps Kaira's dad would be able to talk some sense into their daughter. She had always been close to him and listened to him. Yes, Mrs. Sharma decided. She would speak to Dev about it right now! She had tried to broach the subject with him several times in the last two months but he had always fobbed her off telling her to give Kaira some time and space. But enough was enough! Time and space be damned! She wanted to know what was going on with her daughter. And she would make Dev talk to Kaira and find out.

"Dev! I want to speak to you, right now!" Mrs Sharma marched into the room where her husband was watching a cricket match on television.

"What is it, dear?" he asked, turning down the volume with a patient sigh. His wife was in one of her moods, he realized.

"Well, it's Kaira, Dev. What's going on with her? And don't give me this nonsense about giving her space and time. She has just shut herself up from the outside world. How long can this continue?"

Dev stared at his wife. "Leave her alone, Tara," he said wearily.

"Why should I leave her alone? She's my daughter. I have a right to know what's going on in her life. Has she confided in you?"

"No," Dev replied, taking off his glasses and rubbing his eyes. "She hasn't. But I think I can guess what's wrong."

"What is it? Tell me at once! Is it some boy? Is this why she's behaving like this? But if she likes someone, I won't object. She can marry him. I just want her to be happy..." Tara's voice trailed off as she stared at her husband.

Dev shook his head. "It's not a boy, Tara! It's a girl! It's Joe to be precise."

"Joe?" Tara Sharma shook her head puzzled. "What's Joe got to do with all this? She's just Kaira's friend, that's all."

"No, Tara, I don't think so. She isn't just Kaira's friend. She's far more than that. I think they are in a relationship! I am not absolutely sure, of course. I have just pieced this together from what you've told me about your visit to Kollam, the strange conversation between Kaira and Joe, Kaira's hasty departure, and her behavior since she's returned."

"No, no, no! A thousand times no! You have got it all wrong! It can't be! I can never accept that! Anything but that! What will people say? We will be disgraced."

"But if that's what makes Kaira happy, then we will have to accept it, won't we?" Dev pointed out gently.

Tara sank down on the sofa beside her husband, shaking her head in disbelief. "Are you sure?" she whispered.

Dev shook his head. "Kaira hasn't said anything to me. I'm just guessing."

Kaira walked into the room just then. "Ma, Papa, there's something I want to tell you," she said.

Dev nodded. "Go ahead, Kaira," he said gently.

"Well...I know this will come as something of a shock to you, and believe me, the last thing I want to do is hurt you, but the thing is, well... Joe...Joe and I..." Kaira's voice trailed off as she stared at her parents helplessly.

"It's alright, Kair," Dev said walking up to his daughter and hugging her tightly. "No matter what it is, we will always love you and stand by you."

"Oh, Papa," Kaira said, sobbing as she clung to her father. "I have tried. God knows I have tried! But I just can't live without Joe. She means the world to me."

Tara's face softened as she saw her daughter's obvious distress. Placing her hand gently on Kaira's shoulder, she said, "If it's Joe you love, dear, then you should be with her, shouldn't you?"

Kaira stared at her mother in surprise. "You of all people are saying that, Ma! I thought you would never agree. I was so afraid of losing you, both of you, if I made this choice."

Tara Sharma swallowed as she struggled to hide the distaste she was feeling. But she loved her daughter and wanted her to be happy. And if accepting this relationship was what it took, then so be it. She would do so.

"If you love Joe then you should be with her, Kaira," Dev said gently.

"Oh Papa! Thank you! If both of you are in my corner then I can brave anything. I can take on the world if required."

"It's a hard life you are choosing, Kaira," Dev warned his daughter gently. "It won't be easy you know. Society is not so accepting of ... well relationships like this."

"Say it, Papa," Kaira said fiercely. "Use the word – lesbians! Joe and I, we are not abnormal or bad people. We are just wired differently – that's all! I'm just sorry I didn't have the courage to accept this earlier. I just hope it's not too late and Joe will forgive me."

*****

Kaira rang the doorbell and waited impatiently for Joe to open the door and let her in. She couldn't wait to see her again. But the door remained resolutely shut. Where could Joe be, Kaira wondered. It was just seven in the morning. She couldn't have left for work already. Perhaps she was traveling. Or had she left for good! Lost in thought, Kaira made her way to the beach almost unthinkingly. And there by the seashore, she saw a familiar figure staring out at the sea. Silently, she walked up to Joe and stood by her.

"Most people get tired of the sea after some time. To them it becomes part of the scenery. But you are staring at it as if you are seeing it for the very first time," Kaira whispered softly.

"That's just me missing my artist-friend," Joe said, smiling even as tears welled up in her eyes.

"Can you ever forgive me, Joe?"

"What's there to forgive? I love you – it's as simple as that," Joe said, twining her hand through Kaira's as they stared at the vast blue expanse of the ocean stretching endlessly before them.

"Still? After everything I did?" Kaira asked in a soft whisper.

"Always," Joe replied, putting her arm around Kaira's shoulder and leading her back home.

About the Author:

Zia Marshall holds an MPhil and PhD in English Literature. She is a Learning Designer and Communication Specialist skilled in performance and competency development for personal and professional growth. She creates context-sensitive, solution-oriented e-learning, blended learning, and mobile learning programs for corporate houses like Wipro, Infosys, HCL,

DHL and also for the education sector. She is skilled at applying instructional psychology to learning environments and aligning learning programs with business goals and strategies. She has designed and written several courses deploying life skills, communication skills and skills in dealing with workplace issues. She has also conceptualized and designed products and solutions across multiple industries and verticals such as banking and finance, business logistics, management coaching, performance management, software training, product training, process training and sales and service training. She has worked extensively in the K-12 sector to transform conventional textbook material into story-based multimedia solutions and feedback-oriented assessment banks. Her articles have been published in

http://www.selfgrowth.com/,
https://elearningindustry.com/,
http://havingtime.com/,
https://overcomingms.org/community/blog/.

OUT OF TUNE

by Annina Lavee

We'd all agreed; we'd all emailed; we'd all seen the photos online. We gathered in Ville Pieve a small village outside of Lucca, Italy at a five-hundred-year old villa in early June.

"The damp smell is from a month of rain," said the owner, Mr. Tornetore.

"Mold," said Sandra.

"It's a five-hundred-year old house and it's been renovated. There is no mold. I assure you."

"Mold. My mother is ill from mold. I can smell the mold. It's mold," said Sandra.

Amanda, Susan, Janice, Sandra, Richard and I had surrounded Mr. Tornetore on the great lawn in front of the villa. "If you open the windows and air it out the smell with evaporate," said Mr. Tornetore. "If you run the heaters in each of the rooms the dampness will go away."

We could smell the rosemary, basil and cilantro growing in an herb garden a few steps away. He'd furnished the house with antiques of its era. The outside was painted a leaf green, with white trim, with wooden shutters on all the windows.

Sandra leaned over, her mouth against Richard's ear. "Mold," whispered Sandra. "We can't stay here." Then to Mr. Tornetore, "And there's no bathroom en suite to the bedroom."

"En suite," he said, "surely you understand it's a five-hundred-year-old house. There are no bathrooms next to the bedrooms, but there are three newly renovated bathrooms."

Mr. Tornetore adjusted the glasses on his nose that had dots of sweat.

"But on-line it said it was en suite," said Sandra.

"No, not to the bedroom," said Mr. Tornetore. "I don't understand where you saw it on-line?"

"We won't stay," said Richard. His voice was full volume, strong.

"My friends will not stay and my birthday is ruined," said Amanda. Susan handed her a crinkled tissue. "It's a disaster. She blew her nose."

We'd gathered here for Amanda's fifty-fifth birthday.

Mr. Tornetore's smile sunk. His eyes looked moist. "I'm sorry," he said. "It's been raining for a month. What can I do? There is no basement; it's built on the soil. I have other properties. I'll see if something else is free. I'll call you."

We four women agreed to stay. The couple agreed to stay the night to try the house. The owner agreed to give back a portion of the money if they didn't stay and would call. The seven bedrooms were all off the main room on the second floor, where two grand pianos sat. My fingers ran over the keyboard. Clunk, chink, out of tune. I tried the second piano, with sounds like screeching birds. There was a third piano on the first floor in the smaller sitting room, also out of tune.

The following morning there was no hot water in the bathrooms. The gas tank lived in the entrance hall outside the kitchen.

"What else can go wrong," asked Amanda?

"Maybe it's the light," said Susan.

"Probably it's the light," said Janice.

"Yes, more than likely it's the pilot light," I said.

"It's the light," said. Mr. Tornetore who came and relit the pilot light from a cigarette lighter he carried in his pocket.

Richard and Sandra came downstairs into the kitchen later that morning.

"The bed is too short," said Sandra.

"The mattress is too short," said Richard.

"And the bed is too soft."

"Oh, you mean the mattress is too soft," I said.

Mr. Tornetore did not smile but he did not frown. His face was almost blank, which under the circumstances I thought was a hard thing to do. He returned the agreed amount of money to Amanda. "I cannot find another empty place for you; it's the soccer finals and everyone is visiting. What do you choose to do? Will you stay?"

"I'll call," said Amanda.

"I'll wait for your call," said Mr. Tornetore.

"He's a nice looking man," said Susan.

Janice shrugged.

"He's a nice-looking man," I said.

Two days later, after the four of us visited Cinque Terre, the five towns along the Ligurian Sea, known as the Italian Riviera and a drive in the countryside we found a note taped to the door. Why are you still here? You do not like the villa. Call me. Later that night Amanda called Mr. Tornetore.

"He doesn't understand why we're still here," Amanda said.

"Didn't we agree with him that the four of us stay," I said.

"We said we'd stay, it's just Sandra and Richard who left. I think he's confused or angry," said Susan. Janice nodded in agreement.

That night we went out to a local restaurant for a glass of wine.

"I think Richard and Sandra should come back to stay," said Amanda.

I stared at her for a couple of moments. Did she really say that? "But they were here and didn't like anything about the place," I said.

"Maybe they'll change their mind."

The following morning Amanda joined Sandra and Richard for breakfast at their hotel. Susan, Janice and I met her later.

"They wanted their money," said Amanda.

"And?" I said.

"They just wanted their money."

"Did you give them their money," asked Susan?

"No, just in case Mr. Tornetore changes his mind and wants more money."

"Do you really think he would ask for money back? I said.

"I don't know," said Amanda. "I'll send them the money after I get back home."

"My head hurts," I said.

"I have some aspirin, Susan said.

"Thanks, I'm ok," I said.

Three days later there was another note on the door from the owner. "I have not been able to reach you. I will try again." Amanda was having trouble with her phone. "I think he wants more money," she said.

A meeting was held in the kitchen on the first floor next to the dining room. "We're going to drive Susan to Pisa for her 7am flight," said Amanda.

"I would have liked to be asked," I said,

"You're being difficult," she said.

Janice nodded.

"I'm just saying," I said. "I would have liked to be asked rather than told."

"He's coming tomorrow morning and I'm afraid he wants more money."

"Maybe he doesn't want more money? What if we tell him we don't have more money?"

"He'll block the gate."

"I don't think he'll block the gate. What makes you think he'll block the gate?" I said. "He doesn't appear to be that kind of guy."

"You're being difficult," said Amanda.

"I just don't think he'll block the gate. Why don't you ask him if he wants more money? I don't understand."

Amanda sat there silent. "Up at 3:30am, "she said.

"Up at 3:30am?" I said. "But..."

"See you in the morning," Amanda said. She went up to bed.

I tossed and turned all night.

The car pulled into the Airport Galileo Galilei just outside of Pisa Italy. Amanda was the driver, Janice was in the passenger seat, Susan and I in the rear seat. A week earlier I had been banished to the back seat from a misread of the map of Italy, in my memory a small mishap that caused the banishment. I had offered to be the navigator for a reason. Easily nauseated in a car but less so in the passenger seat, even less so in the driver's seat but I was certain Amanda was never going to let me drive, so I offered to be navigator. The first couple of days were fine then I made that error in my reading of the map and almost got us slightly off-course. A violation, banished to the back seat. The windows were closed, the air stagnant, my body swayed, my stomach sloshed.

"Ok if I open the window?" I said.

"No," Amanda said.

I thought she was deaf in one ear but apparently, she was capable of hearing me in the driver's seat over the car engine. Mistake number two for me. This was just the beginning or the end anyway you'd like to look at it. "I'm easily nauseated," I said to Susan. She either ignored me or didn't hear me. My hand moved to the window crank, the old-fashioned window crank in this car rental. I rested my hand there, leaned my body. One minute, two minutes and then with the slight shift of weight the window came down a tiny bit, just enough to let in some air. No one seemed to notice. I breathed deeply.

But that was a week ago and now we were near Pisa, arrived at 7am so Janice could catch her flight out of Italy. We had left the villa at 4:30am in the morning. Ordered to pile into the car and drive by Amanda who held the car keys. After dropping Janice at her destination I said, "So we're going to see the leaning tower now."

"No," Amanda said.

"But we're so close to Pisa. We can be there in five minutes."

"I don't want to get caught in traffic in Pisa."

"Who cares if we get caught in traffic. What's the emergency? We've been up since 3:30am and we won't even see the leaning tower? C'mon."

Amanda shook her head.

"You're kidding," I said. "I'll drive." I had gotten an international driver's license specifically for the trip. Amanda had said it was a good idea back then.

"The rental car is in my name. It's my insurance. You're not driving." She dangled the keys in her hand.

"But we're so close. We're practically in Pisa." I eyed the keys; could I grab them?

"We're driving back to Florence."

"I'm not much of a tourist but here we are in Pisa. "I want to see the leaning tower of Pisa," I said. "I want to see the tower." If a human could become a twister, I would have spun wider and wider, exploded into a ball of fire.

On the ride back to Florence, Susan was in the passenger seat with Amanda, the driver. I was in the back seat leaning hard on the window crank seeking air.

About the Author:

Annina Lavee teaches screenwriting at the University of Arizona. Her work has appeared in the online Literary Journal Brevity Sandscript, The Awareness Journal, The Mountain Eagle and the Desert Leaf. She has received grants from the Arizona Arts Commission and the Tucson Pima Arts Council and was a Finalist in the Arizona State Poetry Contest-Jorie Graham judge in 2003. She attended the Squaw Valley Community of Writer's program with scholarship and was a semi-finalist for the 2014 Tucson Festival of Books Contest.Lavee worked in film production in New York City including as producer of the short film/video unit at Saturday Night Live.

ABBY'S GOODBYE

by Sharon Frame Gay

Abby saw the news on Facebook. Todd Conway died last night. The funeral will be held Saturday at The Church of the Woods in Deer Ridge. In lieu of flowers, mourners are asked to donate to the Heart Association.

She pushed back from the computer and stood up, paced in circles, sat down again, tried to find her breath.

Todd gone. After all these years. Her first, and if truth be told, only love. The first man to enter her body, weave fingers through her hair, peer into her eyes until he knew every striation in the iris, every stroke of the hand that made her pupils dilate.

The man Abby was meant to be with for the rest of her life.

Only it didn't work out that way. It was supposed to work out that way, damn it, but Todd paid no attention to the law of the Universe and broke her heart instead.

She sat back in her chair, touched the screen with a finger, read the rest. Sal Higgins, an old high school friend, related that Todd keeled over at the local A & W while waiting for his burger and shake. A swift and massive heart attack. Sal saw the whole thing. Said when he fell, he still held on to the shake, and it landed perfectly on the floor, not a drop spilled.

Abby and Todd were high school lovers, sewn together in the tight knit community of a little town in Iowa. In the soft cocoon of their small school, they had already finalized life's plans, and to Abby the cool metal of Todd's high school ring on a chain around her neck was as much a done deal as the sun rising in the East. They breathed the same air, knew the same

people. Before long it was difficult to know where Abby left off, and Todd started. For four years, their love reigned supreme, cast in a tableau with other young lovers whose only ambition, it seemed, was to merge, marry and breed.

There was the usual small town high school pregnancy scare. Abby walking the corridors of school with her girlfriends surrounding her, belly bloated beneath the zipper of her jeans. And Todd had his warriors - fellow jocks who huddled with him on the football field, whispering and conjuring up frightening images of baby blankets and swollen wives. Todd was with her a week later when Abby felt sick and ran into the women's room at Henson's Dollar Store, found blood in her panties. He stood outside the door and heard her let out a whoop, and later told her he nearly fainted with joy.

Was that the first clue? Was he already feeling the loops and threads tighten? Or was it later, when they both went to State University together.

Sal said on Facebook that his wife Loren was with him at the time. Thankfully their kids were at softball practice. Abby's cousin Brad, the local cop, was first on the scene and performed CPR, but Todd was already gone.

Comments poured in. Old friends said they were coming home to Deer Ridge for the funeral. People already making plans to meet at the local steak house on Friday night. Abby could almost feel eyes shifting towards her through the internet, wondering. Would she be there?

Abby would never forget the day Todd broke up with her. It was early spring. Their junior year at State. He asked her to skip classes and go out to the lake with him.

The air was chilly, blowing frothy waves up against the shore. They sat atop a picnic table, huddled under an old quilt. Abby reached over, stroked his thigh. He took her hand, held it still. She looked up, puzzled.

"Abby, Babe, I don't know how to say this, so I'll just come right out with it. I need to move on. It's not that I don't care about you, but I don't think I love you enough. Not in the way people are supposed to love each other if they're going to be married. It just doesn't feel right anymore." Todd looked away, tears in his eyes, his hand shaking.

As many times as she tried over the years, Abby could not remember the rest of the conversation, what the sky looked like, what she said, nor the drive home. What she remembered were the years after that, the years where she shut herself off from romance, watching friends marry and have families, but she remained apart, bemused, as though one foot were in this world, another in a world she only dreamed about.

Her downward spiral was a thing to behold. Never had a jilted lover grieved so much. Abby dropped out of college, lost weight, grew shaky and unbalanced, did things to herself that was wrong. Tiny cuts at first, then larger slices. Cut her long hair into spiky tufts that looked as meager and lost as her legs in faded jeans.

She fantasized that Todd would come back to her. Everything she did, she did with Todd in mind. How would that impress him? Would he like the new color in her hair? Her small

successes from time to time? Todd was the unknowing muse to decades of sorrow and regret, and the need for revenge. Oh yes, revenge.

In her mind, Abby dreamed of this day. Dead Todd. Closure to the story. Abby standing over his grave, a sorrowful look on her face as she turned and walked away, back to a family, career, proper place in the community. In her imagination, her life was a success story, his that of a slow bloomer crushed beneath the

foot of adult life. It seemed to Abby that his existence held her soul in thrall. Todd had died so many times in her tortured thoughts, that hearing about him now, truly gone - seemed like an anti climax.

#

As luck would have it, Abby was in Deer Ridge years ago for Todd's wedding to Loren. It wasn't planned. Just a quick trip back home to visit Aunt Edith and help move her to a senior living apartment. Bells rang out from the church around the corner. Abby saw all the cars, the back of a bride as she walked up the steps, veil flowing in the autumn breeze.

"Who's getting married, Aunt Edith?"

A long pause. Then, "Why, I believe it's that Conway boy and Loren Taylor." Aunt Edith gazed nervously down at Abby's wrists, the scars still pink against her skin.

"Oh," said Abby, turning away before Aunt Edith saw the tears springing up. She fluffed a pillow, threw it in a plastic bag, tossed it in the corner marked for the senior home. "Shall I pack

up the kitchen, Aunt Edith?" She smiled at her aunt, trying to remain calm, as she spiraled down a dark drain, swirling in agony, fighting the urge to run down the street screaming.

Loren. Two years behind her in high school. Abby knew her. In a town this small you knew everybody. What happened after high school, Abby had no clue. Did she also go to State? Stay here in Deer Ridge? Unite with Todd after college? Abby wanted to know everything. Every nuance, every moment and detail about Loren Taylor. She strained her memory, conjured up football games and study halls throughout the years, peering into the past to see if there was already a signal, a sign, a toss of the head, a note passed in English class.

In the end, though, it still boiled down to just one thing. Why was she chosen? Why did Todd wait for Loren at the end of the aisle, lifted the veil from Loren's face, brought her home to their wedding bed and cherished her body again and again, giving them children, a home, a purpose.

As if in answer, Abby saw on Facebook that Loren addressed the comments friends had left on Sal's page. The heartbroken widow found time to commiserate with all the sympathetic friends.

"To all my dear friends, please know I have read the comments from every one of you, and am sending you a big hug. Todd was the most wonderful husband in the world. He was the best father any child could ask for, and the light of my life. My first and only love. XOXO, Loren"

First and only love. Abby was stricken. That was HER position in the galaxy. Todd was HERS first, her first and only love. How dare Loren step in, a latecomer in Abby's mind, and grab the title.

Abby poured herself a stiff one, sat in the worn chair out on the porch, watched kids walking home from school. Felt the haunting, familiar ache that she never married, had no children. She rattled the ice in her cup, toasted the sky, took a sip, then another. Walked back into her lonely apartment.

Should she go to the funeral? How awkward would that be? Wear black like Loren, or a simple linen dress? She'd wander in at the last minute, sit in the back pew, keep her head down, ignore the intake of breath and curious stares from friends. No, it would be a mess. Nobody in their right mind would expect her to come. Especially after what happened five years ago.

#

Abby had come home that year for Christmas. She was gazing in shop windows at the last minute, looking for a scarf for her mother, when Todd was reflected in the glass behind her. She turned, startled, and he smiled that same old smile that she had known since second grade.

"Abby" he said, and her chest loosened as though constricted all this time.

He held out his arms for a hug, stepping forward. She smelled the wool in his jacket, the aftershave, saw the crooked front tooth she knew so well, the tooth she had traced with

her tongue over and over for years. A bit of gray in his hair. The gold band on his finger.

Then she burst into tears. Ugly tears. The kind that comes out in ragged sobs, snot running down her face.

Like a person possessed, she chanted. "Why, Todd? Why? What was wrong with ME? Why didn't you love ME?"

He stepped back, shocked. People slowed, then stopped and stared. And still she continued to cry. It was as though the sky opened, a cloud-burst of heartache, raining down on Todd, the sidewalk.

Carrie Anderson, an old classmate, approached her from the crowd, speaking softly, put her arms around Abby and held her close while Todd, mystified and embarrassed, walked away, the echoes of Christmas music in the background.

Later that night in bed at her parent's house, Abby stared at the ceiling. This was all her fault, she thought. Todd was always good to her. He did nothing wrong. She had no place to set her grief. No blame to smear on his memory. He simply didn't love her. All she had were questions. Questions that would never be answered.

Perhaps that is what made it the most difficult. There was no drama. No cheating heart. There was simply no more. Then came Loren. The kids. A life. And while they built a family together, Abby went to live in the big city, found a drab apartment two blocks from work, trudged home every night to the silence that only a lonely soul can hear.

She had never wanted anyone else. Abby seldom dated, never let a man get too close. Her body still hummed from Todd's touch, and she guarded it, kept it sacred, lighting a candle in the farthest corner of her heart and keeping the flame alive with memories.

Abby had tried therapy, tried expanding her horizons, but nothing seemed to bring her out of the abyss she dove into long ago. It was painful. It was sad. She plucked at the threads of her thoughts over and over again, feeling shame and heartache. And a vast yearning.

With effort, Abby reached over and turned off the computer. Held her hand above the mouse, poised to pounce on Facebook again, changed her mind. Turned away and walked into the bedroom. There, she took off her clothes, stared long in the mirror, ran her hands in ripples over her body where Todd once touched her, hung her head and wept.

#

Two months later, Abby stood in the Deer Ridge Cemetery alone. It was easy to find Todd's gravesite. The soil was still fresh, bald, the tombstone newly chiseled. Flowers dotted the site, bright against the October sky. Abby set a single red rose right next to the headstone, traced his name with her fingertips.

How ironic, she thought. She was the one who should have died, suffering a hundred lifetimes of loneliness and heartache. Yet here was Todd. He went first. He wasn't supposed to go first. He was supposed to yearn for Abby until they were both ancient, then fall to his knees in grief when he heard of her passing, filled with regret.

But Todd didn't fall. He didn't regret. He did not yearn. He merely died.

Abby peered around, then bent to the headstone, kissed his name with her lips. The granite felt cold and final. She turned away, walked back towards the rental car, stared down at her shoes, scuffed, the laces untied. She thought of home, back in the city. She'd been thinking a lot since Todd died. Perhaps she'll paint the old walls, buy a new sofa, maybe even adopt a cat. Get those boots in Macy's window, replace these worn out shoes. These worn out thoughts.

Looking back at the cemetery, the grave was stark and jarring in the afternoon sun. A maple leaf, fiery orange, sailed in the autumn breeze, landed near her feet. How beautiful the leaves are, thought Abby, as the trees set them free. She reached down, picked up the leaf, held it to her heart. Watched it quiver with each beat. Then let it go.

About the Author:

Sharon Frame Gay grew up a child of the highway, playing by the side of the road. She has been internationally published in over fifty anthologies and magazines including BioStories, Gravel Magazine, Fiction on the Web, Literally Stories, Lowestoft Chronicle, Thrice Fiction, Literary Orphans, Indiana Voice Journal, Crannog Magazine, and others. Her work has won prizes at Women on Writing, The Writing District and Owl Hollow Press. She is a Pushcart Prize nominee. You can find her on Amazon Author Central as well as Facebook as Sharon Frame Gay-Writer.

THE PHILOSOPHY OF IRONY IN GREEK CULTURE

by Dimitra Tsourou

This article stems from my dissatisfaction with the available interpretations of irony in Greek culture. A further difficulty in understanding "Greek irony" results from the inability to express its full meaning when translating from Greek into other languages. The main purpose of this article is to clarify the particularity of each type of irony and to draw conclusions about its significance in Greek culture.

WHAT DOES IRONY MEAN?

The multiple forms in which irony appears in Greek culture do not allow for a single definition. From Homer and the Tragedians to Socrates and Plato, irony has been employed in various ways; however, all instances of irony entail a contradiction or antithesis between words and meanings, acts and results, illusive and objective reality, expectations and outcomes.

DRAMATIC AND SITUATIONAL IRONY

The most famous type of irony is "dramatic irony". The term was coined by C. Thirwall in 1833 and has been consolidated since. Dramatic irony appears in two forms: verbal irony and situational irony. "Dramatic verbal irony" is found mostly in the Tragedians, and occurs when the characters use words whose meaning is ambiguous to the audience. A clear example is in Sophocles' "Oedipus the Tyrant" when the old soothsayer visits the king. Oedipus ridicules the man because he is blind, and the outraged Tiresias tells the king that, while he can see, he is "blind" to the truth. When Oedipus becomes blind, he finally understands the meaning of the old man's words.

Artful and articulate, Homer, the author of The Iliad and The Odyssey, was adept at using "dramatic situational irony" – a form of irony that stems from the plot itself and occurs when the characters ignore what the audience already knows. Essentially, it is based on the antithesis between ignorance and knowledge. When Odysseus and Telemachus meet, Odysseus's son is unable to recognize his father in disguise. However, the audience knows everything.

In this form of irony, characters are not able to understand their situation and thus act contrary to logic. The outcome of this ignorance is that the character pursues and eventually expedites his/her self-destruction. Oedipus, for instance, insists on discovering Laios' murderer, without realizing that he is searching for himself – a detail that the audience already knows.

IRONY IN PHILOSOPHY

The multilinear dimension of irony does not end here. In the philosophical sphere, irony takes on a different usage. When Socrates opens a dialogue, he feigns ignorance of the issue in question, challenging both others and his own intelligence. Socratic irony is hence based on the idea that a man feigns ignorance in order to elicit responses from his discussants or to steer the dialogue in a certain direction.

Socrates' conscious statement of ignorance, in conjunction with his deep thirst for knowledge and his belief in lifelong learning, explains why Plato envisages such a strenuous educational system in his "Republic". Plato's use of irony, meanwhile, is revolutionary in many respects. The oxymoron inherent in Platonic irony is that truth emerges from myth. Thus, the paradoxical narration of "The Allegory of the Cave" is transfigured into a logical, realistic, cruel truth about the human condition. It is a conscious choice by the philosopher to show that the myth is in fact the truth. Plato achieves this with eloquence, avoiding pompous expressions or platitudes. His myths are written in simple Greek, not the language of philosophers, and are distinguished by a lack of technical terms. Plato's fluency and simplicity are two virtues that make his writings attractive and readable, even to newcomers to philosophy.

CAVAFIAN IRONY

There is a long history of irony in Greek culture. The internationally renowned poet Constantine Peter Cavafy used irony as an essential tool in his poems. Many have characterized him as a modern philosopher, with irony as the protagonist of his "philosophical" poems. At times, he uses Homeric irony; at others, dramatic irony. The astonishing feature of Cavafy's irony, however, is the unique way that it conveys his message to his readers. In his poem "Waiting for the Barbarians", Cavafy presents a whole community looking forward to their surrender, anticipating the Barbarians' mercy and a return to the simple life. All the leaders, kings, legislators and judges are ready to relinquish their authority to the Barbarians. However, the Barbarians never appear, and the people's expectations are dashed: the irony is created through refutation. Irony is also used in the poem "Alexandrian Kings", when Cavafy implies that there is no value in impressive structures. In her ambitious ceremony, Cleopatra apportions all the territories once conquered by Alexander the Great to her children in an attempt to stupefy the Alexandrian kings. However, the audience already knows the fate of both Cleopatra and her son, and can see the futility behind the lavishness. The poem's beautiful images thus leave a bitter taste.

CONCLUSION

In the modern era, we experience every form of irony. Irony has become more topical than ever in this period of endless relativism and simulated realities where the boundaries between the fictive and the real are increasingly blurred. Irony uncovers the human illusion in every context and in every form. Irony in Greek culture is thus not merely a tool of philosophy or poetry. Rather, it is a philosophy in itself, an ideology, or even a state of being. At times, a sense of unexpectedness, human fragility, self-harm or illusion emerges; at others, irony reveals the absolute un-idealized truth at its most naked and occasionally cruel. The diachronic meaning of irony encompasses the full spectrum of human nature, from naivety to tragedy. In these postmodern, ungrounded times, irony reveals the power of realism.

About the Author:

Dimitra Tsourou was born in Athens, Greece, in 1983. As a qualified Secondary Teacher, Dimitra has a considerable experience teaching Classical Greek, History, Latin, Greek Literature and Creative Writing. She studied Classics and majored in Greek Literature. She also specialized in European History and Political Science. During her studies, she participated in the programme "Balkan Crossroads" pertaining to human rights and peace-building strategies undertaken by the Columbia University. She was awarded a diploma with distinction in Freelance and Feature Writing and in English History from London School of Journalism. She lives in the UK and she works as a Greek Language teacher and writer.

HE LOVES ME, HE LOVES ME NOT

by Michele Sprague

Twenty years ago I couldn't get enough of him. We talked for hours and never ran out of things to say. We greeted each other with anticipation, smiles and lust.

I was 18 then. Putting stock into childish games, I used daisies like people use Ouija boards – as a tool to search for answers. With a pull of a petal I said, "He loves me." Then I pulled the next petal and said, "He loves me not." I continued pulling petals one-by-one until the last petal revealed the answer. If I didn't like the answer, I started the game over with another flower.

In the meantime, our friendship grew. We fell in love and married. On our wedding day he looked lovingly into my eyes and said, "I'm going to make you so-o happy."

I remember some of the good times we shared together. He took me to the botanical gardens and served as my chief photographer; he woke in the middle of the night to help me with a computer program so I could meet my story deadline; and he surprised me with a decorated Christmas tree when I was too depressed to celebrate after my friend passed away.

Nineteen years passed. Our king-size bed, which was once a marital playground, provided distance and loneliness. His body hugged the edge of the right side of the bed; mine hugged the left. The snoring he found cute when we were first married annoyed him.

I didn't remember the last time he said he loved me. Come to think of it, I didn't remember the last time I told him. We didn't laugh together anymore. We rarely went out as a couple, except for an occasional movie and little conversation. The bulk of our activities involved our children.

I remember the early days of our marriage. Just seeing him brought a smile to my lips. I actually enjoyed getting up at 5 a.m. to fix his breakfast and spend quiet time together. Now, I can't remember the last time I fixed an early morning breakfast for him.

And I remember seeing the lit porch light when I returned home in the evening. To me, it represented my home, which was filled with love, comfort and security. It represented coming home to him – the man I dearly loved. As the years passed by, the porch light dimmed. The house no longer felt like a home – it was cold and lonely.

Time moved swiftly from those early, carefree days before our children and advancing our careers. We've drifted apart as if on separate ships to distant countries. And we no longer spoke the same language.

Most nights he retired at 9 o'clock. I was up with the kids, who were winding down. Then I'd retire about midnight. To be fair, he went to bed early because his work day started at 5 a.m.

We spent too much time away from each other – not enough time really listening to each other, taking walks, indulging in playful behavior… We spent very little time being friends, companions, lovers; and almost no time that said "I'm so glad I married you."

The house was very cold. It felt as if oxygen was being sucked out of it. I played the flower game, which I haven't played in 20 years. "He loves me. He loves not." The last petal indicates he doesn't love me. So, I tried the game again but with a different question – "Should we stay together? Should we part?" I cried.

About the Author:

Michele Sprague is the author of the book, "Single Again 101," and wrote hundreds of stories for magazines and newsletters. Sadly, Michele and her husband divorced. Fifteen years later she remarried and lives in Michigan. (portfolio.michelesprague.com)

KINDER-WHORE

by Deanna M. Lehman

(an excerpt)

I was born into a world of darkness and my mother was the moon. Cold and unsmiling, she stood illuminated by her man of the moment, many faces changing throughout the passage of time. How I longed for your love! How I waited for your acceptance. All in vain. The stars around you are the tears I've shed, wavering brightly and already long dead by the time they're perceived. My mother. My Mary. My unrequited love. My betrayer.

I remember the day they took me away. A caseworker arrived at my house. Her name was Diane Solembrino. I remembered social workers taking me to foster care before, so I was suspicious. The last time I was in foster care, it had been with a young, plump woman in a trailer who gave me a chewy hamburger on white bread that I didn't want to eat. I was scared of her because she spanked her daughter in front of me hard, making her cry. I stood in petrified horror and she looked at me and asked, what's wrong? Why are you hurting your daughter, I asked. My mother never spanked me. I'd never seen anyone spanked before. I thought the woman would maybe hurt me too. I wasn't even her daughter. She was being bad, the woman explained patiently. But I'd seen no wrong doing and stayed silent and far from the woman's grasp, which made her sigh. I was in this home not long. Maybe a few days or a week or two. I can't remember. I was too young to have a sense of time and didn't even know how old I was. Maybe three, maybe four. But I did remember the feeling of sadness and not belonging.

Why was the social worker here today? I didn't know that my mother was abusing and neglecting me and that her relatives kept turning her in to the State. I only knew that I loved my mom and didn't want to be taken away. While the adults were talking, I crept away and burrowed behind the curved back of the couch in the dark living room seeking the solace of shadows. I could hear my heartbeat as I half held my breath and tried not to move. I watched the bright circle at the end of the tunnel. Maybe they wouldn't find me. But the sofa was pulled away from the wall and I revealed with nowhere left to hide. The caseworker kept saying that I needed to leave with her. She had carrot red hair cut into a bob with a direct, serious gaze. I don't want to go, I said. She was calm but firm in her insistence. My mother wouldn't look at me. She spoke only to the caseworker in a steady, unintelligible stream of friendly words. A brown paper bag with my name, Deanna, written in black marker, was handed to the caseworker with a daisy drawn underneath my name like I was going somewhere fun, not away from my mother forever. I was handed my stuffed teddy bear Timmy, who I held tightly under my chin and over my heart. Diane took my hand. My mother didn't hug me as she said her final words to Diane. Why did she seem cheerful? It was like she was already serenely separate from me. I hesitated, waiting for her to say goodbye but she ignored me and directed Diane to watch out for the motorcycle, which was parked inside the enclosed porch, on her way out. Uncertainly I left with Diane. We passed Uncle Steve on the way out. He was just arriving to visit with my mother. He said goodbye as we passed each other on the porch.

It was winter, after Christmas sometime and already dark outside. There was no snow, only black skies with naked tree branches dancing. A strong wind blew, licking the cooling tears from my cheeks sideways in liquid streaks as I squinted against it. I could see the Christmas lights strung up on houses in rainbow colors. They swelled to spiky, bright blossoms as tears welled and then contracted to their original pinpricks of light after they overflowed. Over and over again. I had no idea where we were going or why. I sat in Diane's cold, strange car as we drove off into darkness. I cried and asked why I needed to go with her. She said I had to come with her and nothing could change that. I was distracted by looking through the windshield because I'd been on very few car rides in my life. My mom and I mostly walked places, when we went anywhere at all. I couldn't stop the tears from slipping down my cheeks, as houses smeared by outside taking me farther and farther away. Diane said it was for the best.

We arrived at 5721 Adams Avenue in Ashtabula, Ohio. A woman opened her porch screen door to let us in. Well hello there! She was middle aged, with her brown hair pulled atop her head. She led us into her living room where an older man was seated. He folded his newspaper, set it aside and smiled welcomingly. They were introduced to me as Arthur and Sophie Cave. The couple received me with concerned cheerfulness, voices strangely musical, as I stood in their living room eying them warily. Diane handed over my brown bag, told me I'd be fine and said her goodbyes, then left me with these strangers. The door shut and they both looked at me. Mrs. Cave asked if I'd be happy staying with them. I promptly said no, that I didn't want to stay, that I wanted to go home to my mother and baby brother. I held my teddy bear tightly. I trusted that Timmy would help me through all this. He was a living creature to me, silent and watchful with gray, matted fur and unblinking brown eyes. He was my sibling and confidant, soft and soothing to my cheek. Uncle Jimmy won the bear at a carnival and tried to gift it to my mom. She didn't want it though, saying it was cheap. Why don't you give it to Deanna? Uncle Jimmy handed him to me with a small smile. The bear was

snowy white with a light blue ribbon tied round his neck. I knew he was a boy because of the baby blue ribbon, which I asked to be taken off because it had a stiff plastic look and feel I disliked. I didn't know any names, so I wanted to name him Jimmy after Uncle Jimmy in appreciation for the gift. But he said that was his name, so why not Timmy instead. I liked the way it sounded like his name and happily agreed. He was my only toy and very solemn looking because his tiny, tipped over red D of a mouth was unsmiling, his brown gaze ever direct. How many tears had his fur absorbed over the years, changing it into nappy, darker and dingier salt-encrusted shades of gray? Some areas worn bald from being loved overmuch. He never complained and his watchfulness was unwavering. At least he was with me. Mrs Cave opened the paper bag and removed a couple clothing items, a row of cookies in a sandwich bag and a black plastic comb. Is that it, she exclaimed questioningly. She couldn't believe my mother packed so little. These are junk, she said with a wrinkling of her nose, setting the cookies aside to throw away.

Mrs. Cave told me I'd be a very pretty girl if only my hair were combed. I didn't want her to comb my hair because I worried that meant I'd have to stay. That's okay, I said, I have to go home soon, so you don't have to. I felt an exasperated despair, like I was unsuccessfully negotiating with kidnappers. Mrs. Cave asked to comb my hair again, but so nicely that I went along with it, not knowing what else to do. She tried working out the snarls in my shoulder-length hair. I endured her combing awhile. Mr. Cave watched beaming warmly at me. Mrs Cave finished up and then offered me some hot cocoa with marshmallows. I'd never had that before but she said I was in for a treat. She went off to heat the cocoa in the kitchen, leaving me alone with Mr. Cave in the living room.

Mr. Cave was sitting in his brown leather reclining chair, his feet up holding a newspaper. He had a big round belly and reminded me of a teddy bear. He wore glasses and a friendly smile, dark stubble standing stiffly on his cheeks. Come sit with me, he invited, moving his newspaper aside and patting his lap. This scared me and I stood frozen before him. I thought he wanted to play with me. Uncle Jimmy was the only man who'd ever touched me intimately, but he was thin and young and I knew him well. My uncle liked to do things naked with my body but he was my friend and I didn't mind. Nobody else ever really touched me. Not my mom or Big Donnie. Only that one time when Mrs. Munger bathed me. Mr Cave probably wanted to do things with me too but it was awkward because I didn't know him. Also, his tummy seemed so big to me. Maybe he'd crush me if he laid on top of me. I didn't have the words to express these thoughts, being four-and-a-half. So I just stood there hesitating, unsure of what to do. Mr. Cave's smile faltered and I didn't want to hurt this nice man's feelings, so I climbed onto his lap.

I sat stiffly in the depths of the recliner chair, off to Mr. Cave's side, enfolded by the ink-scented, rustling newspaper that he continued reading. I sat waiting for him to do something. Nothing happened. Mr. Cave asked me if I knew how to read. I said yes, thinking that was a good thing to say but when he asked me to point to the words I knew, I realized I didn't know any. I'd never seen a magazine, newspaper or book before but knew about Quik from my strawberry milk. By the time Mrs. Cave came back with the cocoa, I was relaxed. While I was sipping melted marshmallows at the dining room table, I heard a low, whispered exchange between the Caves. Mr. Cave asked his wife if it was possible that I'd been interfered with. I didn't know what being interfered with meant but was paying carefully attention because I felt I wasn't supposed to hear what was said. Mrs. Cave replied, Children's Services didn't say anything about that. I didn't say anything about it either, not having the vocabulary words like penis or vagina or sexual abuse. It would take a gynecological exam at age seven to discover the physical evidence. When questioned about these findings, I broke my promise to Uncle Jimmy that I wouldn't tell our secret and said yes, somebody touched me there. But when pressed for details or emotional reactions to the sexual abuse, I became tongue-tied, embarrassed and silent. Uncle Jimmy was my friend and my feelings about the situation were complex. The psychologist said it was wrong for him to do that but didn't explain

why. The subject of sexual abuse wasn't brought up again in the three years I lived with the Caves. Nor did Mr. Cave ever ask me to sit on his lap again. He was pretty astute, considering how little his intuition had to work with before asking his wife such a question. But to her, the question seemed out of the blue. She hadn't seen my frozen reluctant to sit on Mr. Cave's lap and she didn't mention his concern to my caseworker. I think all children who enter foster care, irregardless of age or gender, should receive complete medical and psychological examinations for signs of abuse, both physical and sexual, so that any therapy needed can be provided as early as possible.

My name's Deanna, it was pronounced Deen-a. That's how my mom said my name. Mrs. Cave kept calling me De-Anna, which wasn't how my name was said. I told Mrs. Cave my real name but she said, no, that's not your name. It's spelled here on the paperwork D-e-a-n-n-a. Deen-a only has one n, so your name's Deanna, she said in the new way. She said she liked the name Deanna because of an actress named Deanna Durbin. She concluded that it was a better name than Dean-a. Soon I accepted it as my own and even grew to prefer its superior phonetic beauty. I was Deanna Cave on my report cards for a couple years, although I was born Deanna Dunford because my mother was married to Dean Dunford when I was born.

I adjusted to my new life with the Caves. My mom hadn't supervised me much, so sometimes my feelings were hurt because I couldn't understand why Mrs Cave got angry at me for little reasons, like playing with the Windex, so beautifully blue and strangely scented with a fun squirt nozzle trigger to squeeze. Before, staying away from the adults was the main rule. I played and did what I felt like and if in the process I made a mess, broke something or hurt myself or others, I got reprimanded afterward and that's how I learned. Here, if I did something I wasn't supposed to do, I often got caught in the act or even right before doing what I desired, which felt strange and restrictive, although I respected it. It even felt like she knew exactly what I was thinking and told me not to do it even though it was still just a newborn thought. Mrs. Cave was amused at my amazement at her ability to predict what I was thinking. You can fool a lot of people but you can't fool mom, she recited. It made me feel she was near magical. I soon realized I could only do what I was instructed to do, not whatever I felt like until it caused a problem. Even specific activity were assigned, giving me more organized and focused play periods which were excellent for skill building. Play on the front porch with your pretend groceries. Here's a ball, go see how many times you can dribble it in a row. Why don't you go play on the swing for awhile? Then I'd go do it until Mrs. Cave told me to stop.

They tried teaching me life skills, like how to spell my name, how to recite our address and how to tie shoes. I didn't always understand why they were doing this. When they presented me with a pile of ugly, worn out, stinky adult shoes to practice shoe tying with, I was bewildered. I didn't want to play with yucky shoes. There was a shapeless tan pair which truly offended my aesthetic sensibilities. Even their eyelets looked stupidly staring with the toes all cracked in creases and tiredly curling tips. I hated them. It took effort to understand how to tie the laces exactly and I didn't want to touch the frayed ends, sometimes gray with dirt. I didn't understand why the Caves were forcing me to sit there until the entire pile had their laces tied. Worse, they stood there watching me and correcting me the whole time. I cried throughout the entire ordeal and hitched a watery, anxious sigh of relief when it was finally over, leaving them both wondering aloud to each other why I was so upset. Won't it be nice to be able to tie your shoes now, they asked placatingly. I just gave them a dirty look and said nothing. But eventually I learned to appreciate the fact that they were trying to equip me with the training that I needed, even if I treated them like they did me an outrageous indignity at the time.

They had me do jigsaw puzzles at the dining room table on rainy afternoons. My favorite featured Robinson Crusoe and had five hundred pieces. It was easy to do the frame using the corners to start out, but my attention wandered filling in the center. I would sit there impatiently, elbow on table, head in hand,

waggling my feet back and forth as they dangled well above the floor, scanning to see where my held puzzle piece went. Mrs. Cave read me two stories from the Little Golden Book series, Jack and the Beanstalk and Mickey Mouse's Picnic, which always made me hungry. I enjoyed the colorful illustrations and the stories soon became familiar favorites.

Mrs. Cave tried to teach me to color in a Scooby Doo coloring book but I had no experience coloring. She was disappointed by my messy first efforts with orange, wild zig zags going well outside the lines. I pressed with heavy intensity, which resulted in a sudden snap and I stared at the two untidy halves. I tried to push them back together bu it wouldn't stay. I wanted a whole crayon but now it was ugly, broken and felt too short. It made me feel disappointed, guilty and sad. Mrs. Cave watched in growing disapproval. I colored with my left hand but she scolded me and put the crayon in my right hand. Why not, I asked. I just wanted to see what it felt like and if I would do better on that side. She gave no real explanation. It's the wrong hand, use the other one. I felt gnawing dissatisfaction because I couldn't figure out why it was wrong. Later in life, I would integrate left-handedness into my repertoire in direct defiance to this memory, becoming partially ambidextrous. But back then, I just used my right hand as instructed. I tried coloring Shaggy again with less pressure, but the color wasn't bright enough that way. I pushed a little harder and snap! Another broken crayon. Two of eight were now broken. Crayons seemed ridiculously fragile. I felt dismayed as Mrs. Cave took the coloring book away saying she'd save it for when I was old enough to use it properly. I felt like I failed.

I only colored at school thereafter, well behind my kindergarten peers in terms of experience. I didn't know how to cut with scissors and had problems using pencils because the lead kept crisply snapping. The teacher wondered why I was going up to the pencil sharpener so many times and my explanation they just keep breaking sounded lame. I wrote such dark markings that if I went to erase a mistake, no amount of rubbing at it seemed to work. I could still see the ghost of it. I tried licking my fingertip and washing the pencil marks away, but it only wet the paper and I ended up rubbing a hole through it when I tried again to erase it. My vigorous erasing made pink smears and usually wrinkled the entire page if it snagged. I was startled to discover that if you erase too briskly, you could burn your fingertip touching the hot spot. I sucked on my finger, near tears from frustration and surprise but the burning sensation quickly faded. My markings were so fiercely pressed that the lead point sometimes tore through the paper, each deliberate stroke left little grated granules of lead which smeared when I went to tidy the page or transferred to gray smudges on my face and clothing. But I was concentrating and trying to control myself with such focus that pressing hard felt natural. The added stress from the bad results increased my anxiety and determination to do better, which in turn caused me to press even harder. I had all these emotional ups and downs. Not that the teacher observed my methods, just the horrible, wrinkled, smeared and holey results which she complained about before my classmates. I wanted to please her so badly. Or at least escape criticism for my clumsy efforts.

I felt like a horrible student compared to the cheerful confidence of my classmates. They didn't seem anxious. They seemed like they were relaxed and having fun. They even talked with each other while I stayed separate not knowing what to say. Why was it so hard for me and so easy for the others? I felt different from them, made worse by the fact that I was the only foster child in the class. They talked of moms and dads and siblings. Their jobs, nice things they said or did or little gifts that they gave them. I had no such details to offer. The Caves said my mother was a bad woman who didn't take good care of me and abused me. I only knew that I loved and missed her and being told she was bad made me miserable. I shrank behind the person sitting in front of me, trying not to be noticed.

But before the stress of starting school, my days from spring to the beginning of fall that year were filled with freedom and play. I'd be busy pulling a little red wagon up and down Adams Avenue with many a noisy clatter. Or

kneeling inside the wagon on one knee and scooting along with the other leg singing, little red wagon painted blue, skip to my lou my darling! I wasn't allowed to go around the block or across the street. Just back and forth along Adams Avenue. We lived near Bunker Hill. Sometimes Mrs Cave took me on a walk to the Stop-N-Shop at the top of the hill, filching mulberries off a large bush along the way. I played outside every day that it wasn't raining. A fresh pile of dirt was purchased and tipped ceremoniously from a wheelbarrow into a rich, loamy pile in the backyard by Mr. Cave. I made mud pies and gingerbread boys, carefully decorated with pebble buttons and dry dirt for sprinkled sugar. I enjoyed getting absolutely filthy. There was a garden with sun-warm tomatoes and a variety of flowers in a rich range of colors. I liked the sweetly scented snapdragons with their purple and white snouts roaring silently at the press of a delicate jaw hinge. There were pussy willows in the spring, light gray and velvety soft to the lips and nose. In the summer a grapevine hung heavy with green and purpling globes of slipskin grapes. There was a sour green apple tree which made me salivate to even look at and a lone raspberry bush growing along the very edge of the back yard keeping the tall peach tree company. There was a tree with a wooden board swing which had a cool, moist clay furrow curved beneath from bare feet. I'd swing as high as I could, protected from the burning sun by the shade singing songs to myself taught by Mrs. Cave. I was happily busy during the day.

At night, I had trouble sleeping. I just wasn't able to. I would play with Timmy, either rodeo rider where my foot was Timmy's bucking broncho or I'd have him do a series of flips, catching him in my hands. Then I would just think and think and think to pass the time. I was starting to love the Caves but still missed my mom and wanted to be with her. I missed my baby brother with his blonde, tousled hair and silly smiles. I'd lay in my bed on the bottom bunk staring at the overhead mattress and tracing the metal lattice diamonds. I just didn't feel sleepy and was put to bed at eight, which felt especially cruel in summertime when it was still light outside. I'd watch the bleeding sunset fade to black, mourning the loss of precious playtime. The nightlight in the hall made everything golden sepia-tinged surrounded by shadow. A Chewbacca piggy bank stood guard by the door, anchored with countless pennies within. I would hear different TV shows turn to nightly news downstairs. Then Mrs. Cave would look in on me before turning in for the night with Mr. Cave in their bedroom across the hall. I was sometimes the last person in the house to fall asleep.

In the dark for many hours, I'd play all the memories of my mom that I could remember. I'd do this nightly because it made me feel closer to her and I didn't want to forget her. I felt if I forgot her then I'd never see her again. I hoped one day she'd take me back home. My mother was thin, with long, straight brown hair past her waist and dark brown eyes. She had a deep tan, so different from my own strawberry-blonde paleness. The 1/4th Cherokee blood was very apparent in her. She was beautiful to me, especially in the soft focus of my memories. Mr. and Mrs. Cave were in their fifties, more like grandparents than parents. My grandmother was younger than Mrs. Cave. I missed my mother so.

About the Author:

Deanna M. Lehman is an author, poet and artist currently residing in Des Moines, Iowa. She is currently represented by the James Fitzgerald Agency of New York City and is the author of Kinderwhore, available through Amazon.

THE EIGHTIES

by Betty J. Sayles

My son was a career Air Force man and while visiting me in northern Wisconsin, he saw 80 acres of woods, swamp and beaver dam that he loved on sight and wanted for a summer home when he retired. There was a vintage house trailer on a large clearing near the road, and with water, bottle gas cooking stove and an outhouse, he could stay there, comfortably enough, during summer visits. With two days left before he was due to leave for his next station overseas, he completed the transaction and owned the land. He left the key to the trailer with me.

I made numerous trips to the "80" that summer. I learned my way about the woods, and while sitting on the bank of the beaver pond watching for beavers, enjoyed dozens of jewel colored dragonflies darting about. I never saw a beaver, but saw a stump and freshly gnawed wood chips.

Under the steps of the trailer lived a nest of bumblebees. I often sat on the steps, basking in the sun, and the bumblebees entered and left their home with no apparent concern or malice towards me. I enjoyed watching them. On the opposite side of the trailer was a pump with deliciously cold water. After a warm walk in the woods, that pump would be my first stop. Unfortunately, some yellow jackets also liked it and made their nest in its spout.

I suppose there's no parallel between the bumblebees and the yellow jackets because one lived side by side with me and we didn't interfere with each other. In the case of the yellow jackets, we both wanted the same spot and that can do dire things to a "Live and Let Live" philosophy. It has, also, been my observation that bumblebees have a placid nature while yellow jackets come at you like a "Spitfire" at war, at least, when you dislodge their nest with a gush of water.

We waged war for a month or more. I still don't know how I came through unscathed, I was threatened often enough, but it's amazing how fast a human can move when the adrenaline is at its peak and he's fighting for something he considers belongs to him. My offense was always the same; I'd give a mighty pump on the handle, and dash for the back door that was only 10 feet away. I'd look through the window and there he'd be glaring at me inches from my face [I swear it was the same one every time, he hated me].

With the nest dislodged, the yellow jackets would hover about for 10 minutes, or so, and then leave, and it would be safe to go out and pump "my" water.

With a week usually elapsing between my visits, the yellow jackets always had a new nest built in the pump spout. Then, one day, I made the dash for nothing, the enemy had departed. I was surprised to find that I was disappointed; after all, my old enemy had been a worthy adversary and our encounters had been exciting. I wondered if they would be back the next summer.

About the Author:

Betty J. Sayles is a retired librarian who has been writing most of her life, but only tried for publication a few years ago. She loves to read, everything from Poe's Raven to Rex Stout's Nero Wolfe. She walks in the woods and writes a poem about it. And she writes about feelings, good and bad.

She has had short stories and poems published in Storyteller, Creative With Words, The Oak, Nomad's Choir, Ultimate Writer, Persimmon's Tree, Spontaneous Spirits, PKA Advocate, Amulet, Mystical Muse, LOS, CC&D, The Enchanted File Cabinet, Conceit, Shemom, Pink Chameleon, PBW, Down in the Dirt, The Weekly Advocet, Van Gogh's Ear, Yellow Mama, Song of the San Joaquin, Better Than Starbucks, Pennine Ink and Stray Branch.

THE HOWL OF AN AMERICAN PSYCHO: An Introspection into the Destructive America
by Vanya Suchan

To raise the notion that the human being reaches for the glamorized "American dream", but remains crushed in her struggle and trapped in a capitalist worldview, we might first examine the works of Ginsberg's beatnick call for the affirmation of life as it appears in his poem, Howl. In his notions, Ginsberg explores the destitution of America and the "best minds of [his] generation [have been] destroyed by madness"(1),"demanding instantaneous lobotom[ies]..."(69). Ginsberg preaches of the all-too American endeavor to meet the demands of the melee of fighting for success in a stratified, capitalist society. Here, Ginsberg expounds on the human being's struggle to exist in fighting for the realization of the "American dream". This incommensurability that lies at the heart of such platitudes destroys the momentum of her becoming who she is and what she initially grasps for in the first place: the forgotten American Dream of life, liberty, and the pursuit of happiness. Ginsberg continually questions the stability of America, inquiring into the nature of the "American dream". The very ideal of the "American dream" commercializes what the human being strives for is that which drives the crushing of her sanity. On my reading and as it appears in the text, the human being ventures for what her true American dream remains as, something destroyed in the process of her enlightenment to reveal the source of true happiness. Here, I would like to bring these thought paths of Allen Ginsberg into dialogue with Bret Easton Ellis' "American Psycho" as a way of opening up a hermeneutic understanding of Howl. The cinematic adaptation, written by Mary Harron and Guinevere Turner, depicts

the mental destruction and the clinging to escapism from what exists as the human being's reality after the confected and dangerously romantic "American dream" comes to fruition. On my reading, the erosion of the human being's spirit, and in turn assimilation into an unnatural, capital and freedom driven existence, ensues in both Ginsberg and Ellis' works. In this way, the polarizing and materialistic idea of freedom, grounded throughout the nation, eradicates that for which Allen Ginsberg fights and stands. As such, the residue of the human being left behind remains her madness, which I insist on understanding as corresponding with that of Ellis' depiction of the cliché realization of the American dream in the film American Psycho: an exaggerated extreme of the American ideal as the creation of freedom fostered in heinous acts of murder.

In exploring there heinous acts of murder motivated by the American dream ideals, the film adaptation of American Psycho follows an elite businessman, Patrick Bateman. As demonstrated in the film, he exists hindered by the binding role as a successful man in a consumer driven society. He prides himself on his wealth, status through his possessions, and physical appearance. Housed in the "American Gardens building on West 81st Street on the 11th floor" his social prestige, although impressive, still leaves him struggling to meet the standards of the social strata of his colleagues. Bateman, routinely mistaken for other men, described as the "boy next door" and " ...a dork...[s]uch a boring, spineless lightweight", struggles with his own masculinity and the fragility of his status. Living wholly obsessed with his self-image and ability to "fit in", he endures a "balanced diet, [and] a rigorous exercise routine" and yet lacks a sense of control. He lives the "American dream", but fails to find pleasures in his routine life, fiancé and luxurious lifestyle. Fabricating an escape from his detrimental regimen of the nine-to-five finds itself in the gruesome killing of his co-workers, prostitutes, and those who impede his success, a pastime that exclusively exists as his only true coping mechanism. Bateman exists in a detached state with his "self" similar to the Ginsbergian human being. Both variations of this human being exist in the distorted idea of the American dream, forced to carry out the life and ideals of an abstracted vision in which from they wish to diverge. In her attempt to survive, she requisitely "fad[es] out in vast sordid movies...picks [herself] up out of basements...stumbl[ing] to unemployment offices" (43). The identity in the private discourse of her and the idea of herself she portrays to the public both are rooted in and juxtaposed to one another. In this way, she remains in a disconnected state with herself, obligated to juggle between the side in which she will present to the public and the side she discloses to herself. Much like the human being, Bateman exists in as Heidegger deems the human being as das unheimlich, the unhomely way in which she dwells estranged to herself, trapped in mediating between a capitalist America and her authentic attunement toward being.

Bateman, existing in what I call an unhomely comportedness, lies collocated to his, if not sterile, dwindling passion of his pneuma, the vital spirit of his being. As illustrated in film, through the character of Bateman, the human being loses herself in her endeavor for commercial happiness. The core of her being lies deprived of the forgotten American dream, becoming an idea, a routine, as she lives "hug[ing] and kiss[ing] America under [her] bed sheets" (127) "while it coughs all night and won't let [her] sleep", the same America that Ginsberg laments. (128) Ginsberg's verdict on the sickliness of America we see epitomized in the character Bateman as he broods on his actuality that "there is an idea of Patrick Bateman, some kind of abstraction, but there is no

real [him]". Bateman flees towards an escape from the tortures of his dying core to an existence of control through animalistic behaviour. The indulgent pleasures of sex and drugs, such as that of his colleagues, inefficiently quenches Bateman's yearning to kill, a symptom of the ailment which afflicts this kind of American society.

Reaching for a diversion from this lifestyle, Ginsberg similarly presents the human being taking on her own methods to reaching an escape from the incarceration of her societal roles that she insists on playing. She takes part in the external pleasures of "drugs... alcohol and cock" (11), a hubristic act in an attempt to reach happiness before she is forcefully shocked herself out of her "natural" ecstasy by Moloch, the canite demon in "Howl". She diverts herself from the constructs of societal norms, extending to the divine in an "ancient heavenly connection"(3) in a moment of flooding freedom, clinging to her daily sojourn. In this way, the human being has the ability to achieve a moment of peace without dragging in the body of the taboo and monstrous lifestyle of Patrick Bateman. Comparable to the human beings diversion in Howl, American Psycho invokes these occuring themes and motifs as well. Throughout the film, drugs, sex, and alcohol exist as a crutch, even a prevailing mechanism for the most elite in the business world. These imperious characters spend their free time worrying about how "good [a] bathroom [is] to do coke in" and a woman "who will satisfy all sexual demands... without being too slutty about things." Their domineering traits, employed by the demands of a competitive and hypermasculine culture, force them to escape to a realm that Ginsbers identifies as a "starry dynamo in the machinery of night" (3), unable to find happiness in their own realities. On my reading, these men, much like the human being, cling to any escape from her actuality and the mockery of her embarrassingly simple existence. She lives detached from her self, existing as "some kind of abstraction...", a conceptual version of who she really appears to exist. Through the human being's process of seeking the fundamental life of the "American dream" she finds herself in a tortured state of being. The shallow ideology that supports the capitalistic "American dream", destructive in nature, embeds itself in her and manifests into a bitter existence. Her "self" and who she once lived as subsists in disunity, emblematic of an eristic existence. Her life is now one of dis-chord and friction between who she wants to be and who she is forced to routinely dwell as and against. She now remains as an imitation of herself, her past ideals forgotten, clocked-out of her pneuma, living solely for the tasks she must complete. Although she has reached a point of supposed success, what was seem-ingly her goal, she remains yearning and pining to bridge her existence to that of the forgotten American dream. In this way, the divide be-tween attaining the "American dream" and the happiness beyond the bounds of that notion exists as a liminal space she cannot cross. Here, the human being finds herself forced to remain trapped by the societal duties of the "American dream" or live detached from this reverie eter-nally. She remains fastened between the two, struggling, possibly even failing to mediate be-tween them. This detrimental life she leads Ginsberg, diagnosing this as "the narcotic haze of capitalism" (51), which blinds her as she takes a proverbial drag from that cigarette of an inescapable and monstrous ideals of a capi-talistic driven democracy. What she was once in awe of now embodies that of her nemesis. She lives howling for those who "bared their brains to Heaven..." (4) and howls for the "ancient heavenly connection"(3) and "though [she] can hide [her] cold gaze, and you can shake [her] hand, [she] is simply not there." In the human being's attempt to sprout form the soil of the forgotten American dream, she di-verges from her once un-tainted desires to a corrupted agenda. Only when she realizes that this seeded perversion has bloomed like a "sunflower...on top of a pile of ancient saw-dust" (4), does she have the choice to escape.

Work Cited

Ginsberg, Allen. Howl. The Norton Anthology of American Literature, W.W. Norton and Compa-ny, 2012. p. 492-500. Print.
Harron, Mary American Psycho. (2000). [DVD].
Ginsberg, Allen. Sunflower Sutra. The Norton Anthology of American Literature, W.W. Nor-ton and Company, 2012 .Print.

About the Author:

Vanya Suchan is a student who attends Lakehill Preparatory in Dallas, Texas where she studies and excels in deep textual analyzation of litera-ture and poetics. Her work mainly focuses on the human being's existence in dialogue with other texts. She hopes to be able to share her work with others and to help readers be as passionate about literature as she is.

FAKE PEOPLE ARE THE BEST ONES

by Cassie Follman

When I was a kid, I was enamored with the world of Pretend. Endless possibilities stretched out before me, and imagining fake scenarios came second nature. Characters squirmed their way into my brain and sunk their teeth into the caverns of my ears. They whispered adventures that I had to write, and refused to leave me alone, like my incessant younger cousin who had just discovered annoying people was the single-handedly most entertaining thing in existence. To please the characters, I would often act out these adventures myself, or through cunning negotiation with my older sister. This tactic usually involved me promising to give her the last piece of tomato pie pizza. I was lucky that her main motivation in life at the time was food, it would have been much more difficult if she had requested something else, like Webkinz, as payment. Those bitches were expensive.

One such situation consisted of my sister and me pretending that we were heroines with magical abilities. While my mom shopped, we ran around Ann Taylor, ducking into coat racks to battle dragons. We stormed upon display sets and dashed into dressing rooms to rescue timid little boys who cowered under their beds.

"Oh, how can I ever repay you?" They begged while sinking to their knees in awe of our amazingness.

"By swearing your allegiance to us and promising that if you are ever in danger, you will call for us." Of course, they always did.

Sometimes my sister would screw up the story by adding in, "And don't forget to tell everyone that I'm the superior sister," or other equally irritating comments that she only said to rile me up.

It worked, too. Her add-ins usually led to me yelling at her for ruining everything by breaking the magic. Not to mention that she had messed up the scene where I was supposed to be crowned The Greatest Heroine of All Time.

Most children have a favorite stuffed animal, my sister's was a terrifying cat, named Fuzzy, that she slept with until she became "too cool", and went to high school. I was never obsessed with a certain object, though that did not prevent my obscene collection of stuffed fluffy white rabbits and black Labrador puppies from storming my bed like a castle and staking their claim there for years. Instead, my Fuzzy manifested from Pretend.

I was addicted to making one character as real as possible. He was formed from photographs and stories told with shiny, melancholic eyes. His hair was messy, dirty blond, his eyes an indeterminate blue. The khakis he wore were tattered, the beer t-shirt had holes he couldn't have been prouder of, and his loafers were destroyed. Huge glasses were perched on his nose. My dad.

He never said much. The comments were small, insignificant. Their structure was flawed, and ideas ran together. They swirled in bubblegum pink and lilac, like the 'potions' I made out of only my mother's finest bath products. Their mere existence made them invaluable.

The words he said were lies, as he was not real. At some point he was, but for my life, he was nothing more than a story. I outlined his image in my head and stared at the crappy brown chair that used to be his. With my eyes squeezed tight, I would put him together one piece at a time.

"Maybe if I stared with enough intent, I could conjure him up into existence." I had whispered to myself on one occasion.

Once, I went out to the swing set behind my house and kicked my legs as hard as I could. My rhythm on the swing was wobbly. I imagined that my extreme height was due to my dad's strong arms sending me flying up, up, up toward the kaleidoscope leaves from the trees in mid-October.

I craved validation from the one person I would never receive it from. On the occasions that we would talk, he fueled my pride. The voice was the hardest part, and I could never get it quite right. I tried different movie stars, attempting to find one that fit. For a while I settled with Ferris Bueller, but I grew frustrated as it didn't sound perfect enough.

Sometimes, I believed my mom thought I was insane, often asking me, "Who are you talking to?"

Out of embarrassment, I never managed to respond further than, "Ugh, no one!"

Pretend was both rewarding and torturous. It was like I was desperately thirsty, and my brain conjured up a glass as a mirage. Then, it filled that glass to the brim with ice cold water. I could almost feel the water running down my throat, putting out the fire. The water would never be mine, as all games have their limitations. Still, for those few seconds when I was able to picture my dad, the thirst was a little less unbearable.

About the Author:

Cassie Follman is an aspiring writer from Philadelphia, PA. She is currently obtaining a Bachelor's degree in History and English, with an emphasis in Creative Writing at Smith College. She has been writing and reading her entire life and has served on the boards for school newspapers and literary magazines.

DERELICT

by Allen Long

I once sat on the floor at a Saturday night party at my friend Rick's house; I was drunk, and Rick unknowingly stood on my legs, sipped a beer, and conversed with a pretty blonde from school named Jane. I'd downed six large plastic cups of Heineken from the keg for two reasons. First, I'd just worked nineteen of the last twenty-four hours as a cook at Pizza Hut, and my legs ached bone-deep, so the brews served as sedatives/painkillers. Second, I'd entered junior high as a crew-cut straight-A widely despised nerd, and now that we were high school seniors, I enjoyed shaking my shoulder-length auburn hair and reminding my classmates I could party with the best of them.

"Rick!" I shouted. "Watch the legs!"

Rick glanced down, laughed, stepped off my pins, and apologized. Jane smiled at me, but I was clear-headed enough to catch the flicker of disappointment in her eyes. I was embarrassed. Jane and I'd been in school together since kindergarten or first grade. Our mothers were friends from college, so Jane came over to play at my house periodically when our mothers got together. My guy-room didn't interest her, so we often went for short walks; we liked each other but were too shy to say much. I had a bit of a crush on her that lasted for years. During our best visit together, we gorged ourselves on delicious green grapes growing on a fence we shared with a neighbor who raised orchids and parakeets. This was a bonding moment for sure, but our only one.

At Yorktown, our high school, Jane and I smiled and said hello in the halls. She seemed poised for a highly successful life: she was attractive, friendly, and down to earth; she was well-liked by her classmates, she held a high rank in student government, and she'd aced her classes and was Harvard-bound. I was happy for her, but I felt a wistful regret that we'd never become closer. I was a smart guy with good prospects, but here I was now, drunk on the floor without the maturity or common sense just to sip my beer socially.

To make matters worse, I caught Wendy Summers looking at me with pity as well. Wendy was a stunner, with long red hair and matching green eyes. Also, she smiled and laughed a lot and seemed like a kind and happy person. I had a big-time crush on her, but I knew she wasn't available. She stood with her boyfriend Frank Delatorre, who was a bit short, but he was deadly handsome with piercing blue eyes and shiny liquid-gold hair.

Luckily, I redeemed myself with Wendy before the school year ended. This was 1975 in Arlington, Virginia, and Wendy and I were both in a psychology class engaged in encounter groups. Our class was divided into four small groups, and Wendy and I were in the same cluster. We were encouraged to tell our peers the basics of our personalities and interests within five minutes. Then each classmate would make honest comments about how he/she perceived that person. The idea seemed to be to identify gaps or a lack of gaps between these two realities. We were encouraged to hug each other at the end of the session to soothe hard truths and our high anxiety levels. Our much-loved teacher, Mr. Lee, circulated from one group to another, monitoring our progress and making sure our comments about one another remained humane.

Wendy said she wanted to become a nurse because she liked helping people; two years as a volunteer at Arlington Hospital had inspired her. Her expression was bright and open. God, I loved her, or I thought I did. When it came time for my comments about how I perceived her, I said, "I think you're very attractive and also full of kindness and positive energy. You'll make a terrific nurse." She smiled, her eyes shiny with gratitude.

When it was my turn to describe myself, I said, "I'm a pretty mellow guy, kind of shy, and I love reading, writing fiction, swimming, playing guitar, and spending time outdoors⬚ in fact, I'm going to Virginia Tech and may end up as a forest ranger⬚ spending time outdoors is very spiritual for me." I pictured myself working contentedly at a remote post in a gorgeous forest and writing fiction in these inspirational surroundings. This never happened⬚ I ended up unhappily working in the business world in expensive California, where we moved to be close to my first wife's family.

In high school, I had three close friends: my buddy Will whom I'd known since first grade, my friend Nick whom I'd met in seventh grade and who shared my passion for swimming and science fiction and horror books/movies, and my pal Craig V. who played guitars with me. Otherwise, I wasn't that well known, so my encounter group mates told me how happy they were to get to know me.

Wendy commented last: "Before today, I thought you were a total derelict, but I can see now you're a smart nice guy who's going to be happy and successful." When the embracing began, Wendy made straight for me and gave me a bear hug. She held me tighter and longer than I expected, and I felt we became friends. Unfortunately, I never saw her again after graduation, despite attending a couple of class reunions. I still think about her, though, especially since I now work as an assistant nurse in an inner city hospital⬚ as it turns out, I, too, discovered a deep desire to help others.

I recently dreamed about Wendy. We were back in high school, and there'd been some kind of natural disaster in Arlington, and we had to evacuate our homes for the night.

Wendy and I ended up in the same shelter, sitting together on a sofa. We were pleased to have each other for company, and when we became sleepy, I put my arm around Wendy's shoulders, and she snuggled into me, leaning her head against my chest. We fell into a deep and contented sleep. This is one of the most peaceful dreams I've ever had.

Okay, so there's a third reason I was drunk at Rick's party. My younger brother Danny and I were physically abused by our parents from the time we were small children until we each entered seventh grade. So I was a bottled up guy who enjoyed uncorking myself now and then. That's why Wendy's friendship hug felt like pure, unadulterated love and why I wanted to redeem myself with Jane.

Jane gave a speech at our graduation ceremony, but I didn't see her at any of the parties that ensued. Soon after, we left for college and lost all contact. However, over the years, I received tidbits of news about Jane from my mom. She graduated with honors from Harvard; she earned a B.A. in art history and debated whether to pursue an art-based career or study law. Her father, who'd abandoned the family when Jane was in elementary school, was a lawyer. She fell into crisis trying to figure out if she really wanted to be an attorney or if she was considering that path to please/impress her father. She put her life on hold and sought therapy. Later, Jane married, and her husband left her. She returned to therapy. Jane dated and then married one of our high school classmates, Jimmy Thornton, and they had two sons.

I was pleased to hear of Jane's triumphs and sad to learn of her struggles. I wished I could help her in some way, but she was on the East Coast, and I was married and living near San Francisco. I don't know why, exactly, but I felt an unusual amount of empathy toward her, perhaps because we'd partially bonded when we'd laughed with crazed abandon as we stuffed ridiculous amounts of jade-colored grapes into our mouths, the sticky sweet juice pouring down our chins. Also, we'd both been somewhat beat up by life.

And I was happy to hear Jane had married Jimmy Thornton because I remembered him as a good-natured kid with a sense of humor. Jimmy was a friend of my buddy Nick and often sat with us at our junior high lunch table. Whenever we got into insult battles, Jimmy might say, "That's pretty big talk for a one-eyed fat man!" A line from the John Wayne movie, True Grit. Or sometimes he'd say, "I've et better men than you with their heads buttered and their ears pinned back!" Source: unknown.

I wondered if Jane ever thought about me, and if she did, was I her grape-guzzling buddy, a derelict, or something else? I suspected I rarely crossed her mind, and if I did, she probably just remembered me as a nice guy she'd known from her pre-college school years.

Shortly after I made plans to attend my thirtieth high school class reunion in Washington, D.C., my mother, who was friends with Jane, called to tell me that Jane would be there as well and wanted my advice about a world-famous and expensive French restaurant in Berkeley where she and her family planned to dine while on vacation. I knew the restaurant and said I'd be happy to pass on a couple of tips. I was excited and curious about seeing Jane.

***

I attended the reunion alone, my beloved second wife Elizabeth having stayed behind in California with our four children. The venue consisted of an insanely crowded bar with French doors opening out upon an expansive lush and fragrant garden. I wended my way to the bar and ordered a Corona with lime. Of my close friends, only Nick was attending the reunion, and I didn't see him, so I strolled the grounds, stopping periodically to sip my brew and chat with classmates I remembered liking. Fireflies flickered around us. After several encounters, I met up with Jane. She looked pretty and elegant in her simple black dress with pearls. We smiled.

Jane said, "It's so wonderful to see you!"

I concurred. Then we spent a few minutes catching up⬚ Jane had ended up working as an art therapist, and she was now a stay-at-home

mom; I was founder and president of a small Silicon Valley high-tech marketing firm. I didn't know it then, but my firm was destined to get wiped out in the Great Recession that began in 2001, and I would become a swimming instructor, a swim team coach and, later, an assistant nurse, all very satisfying "helping" jobs. We briefly discussed our families⬚ I knew Jimmy, of course.

Finally, Jane glanced at me shyly and said, "Did your mom tell you I was hoping you could give me a few pointers about the restaurant?" When I nodded, she said, "Is there any informal way to eat there? I'm afraid the boys might not present the best manners. Also, is there any trick to keeping the price down while still having a good meal?"

Before I could answer, Jimmy rounded a nearby oak, glared at me, and shouted at Jane. "Where the hell have you been? I need you over here with me, now!" He grabbed her arm with surprising force. Jane cried out and broke free.

"You're not doing this!" she yelled. "You don't own me⬚ I'll be there when I finish talking to Allen⬚ don't you even want to say hi to your old friend?"

Jimmy shot me a venomous glance and strode back the way he'd come.

"What's wrong with him?" I said.

"Stress," she said. "He does classified work for the government, and it takes a toll."

Jane's face creased with anxiety, and she trembled. I longed to touch and comfort her. I think she sensed this but was afraid she'd break down if I made contact. Also, touching wasn't in our repertoire.

She forced her face into a bright expression. "So, please, tell me about the restaurant!"

"There're two tricks to it," I said. "Go there for lunch because it will only cost half the price of dinner. Also, eat downstairs versus upstairs because downstairs is less formal, and you should be able to have your sons with you without any hassle."

As I delivered this information, the last of my

a warm glow of satisfaction from helping my friend after all these years. But even as Jane thanked me and turned to join her husband, I knew my gift was like one of the fireflies surrounding us⬚ a brief flash of luminescence besieged by darkness.

About the Author:

Allen Long is the author of Less than Human: A Memoir (Black Rose Writing, 2016). His work has recently appeared in Adelaide Literary Magazine and the Adelaide Literary Awards Anthology 2018. In addition, his memoirs have appeared or are forthcoming in Broad Street, Eunoia Review,and Hawaii Pacific Review. An assistant editor at Narrative Magazine since 2007, Allen lives with his wife near San Francisco.

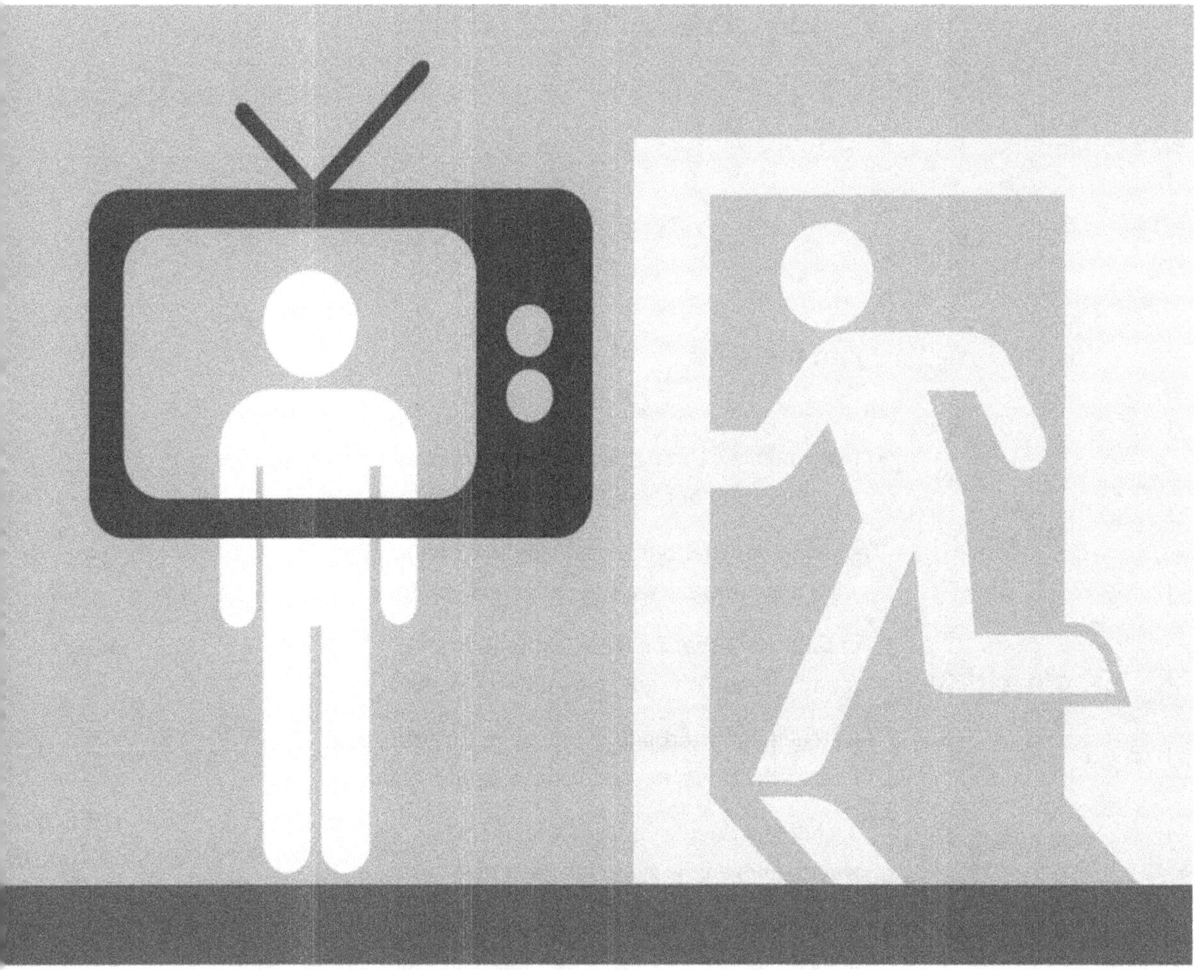

AND THE WIND
by Kevin Gillam

and the wind

the wind blew through us. we were small that
day, there and not. sea was scuffed, frothed, whipped,

smear of land far out where blue skirts blue.
wind blew through us. swept us clean, swept us

of tales and ache. we were lost that day,
found but not. one gull, high up, wheeled and

watched. blew through us. we were song that day,
free on the stave, note then note, spume and

a whiff and dried weed, lick and boom of
waves, nudge of groyne. the wind blew through. we

were sand that day, sand and salt and shell
and curled. we were grain that day. wind through

us. glint of sun off the quilt of brine.
we were small and hope. the wind through us

dust bowl days

it was in April I believe,
on a Sunday. Frankie was

on the veranda, chewing
has 'bacco, spitting and

staring, staring into nothing.
"see how spotty that wheat is

out there?" my eyes take in
swathes of rippling stubble.

"well that short stuff shouldn't be
brindled like that." "Drought turns 18".

that was the header of the
weekly rag. our eyes meet.

"these are dust bowl days". a gob
of his spit folds in gravel

the colour of healing

it's a thick silence,
unrehearsed and accidental,
with the house suddenly empty.
rare, in a home like this –
grand piano, two 'cellos, violin, guitar –
three musicians and a dog,
Bach Chaconnes, Chopin Preludes and
high pitched whines joining 'cello duets

has me thinking though,
about the repositories of silence
because it's been here and waiting,
in the 45 degrees of stairwell, the angle
providing harbour, a balloon of silence
the colour of healing

About the Author:

Kevin Gillam is a West Australian writer, 'cellist and music educator. He has had 4 books of poetry published, the most recent being "the moon's reminder" with Ginninderra Press. He works as Director of Music at Christ Church Grammar School in Perth.

STRANGERS ON A TRAIN

by James K. Zimmerman

Midflight

that old man
because he can't
get his bag down
from the overhead bin

because he can't
unzip it with bulging
knuckles and neuropathic
fingers

because he can't
find the whatever
he was looking for
in it with eyes
that don't see as well
as they should
and thoughts that don't
come so easy anymore

who has too many
chins and bags
under his eyes
and knees and elbows
that don't cooperate
like good children
or well-trained cockapoos

who is chewing chips
with an open mouth
and salted tongue

who is blocking
the aisle so I can't
get by to get
my bag down
from the overhead bin

that old man
may be several years
younger than I am
and not even realize it
until he gets off the plane

and we go home

Strangers on a Train

I want you to pay
attention, see my
wryly dark sense
of humor, cool new
tattoo, awesome
designer shades, 'cause

I like the way you stare
out the window

so I clear my throat
sniff a couple of times
blow my nose
clear my throat again

I want to say look: don't
you see how deep I am?
a sensitive soul? don't you
see I am, y'know,
a poet? so I

riffle through my narrow-
ruled Moleskine with the ribbon
bookmark – 'cause poets
don't use iPads – stroke
my three-day beard, totally
into it, click my pen, chew on it
a little (deep in thought) and

write something profound
and metrosexual but not
too touchy-feely, nuts-
and-berries or emo and

write it big enough so you
could read it if you happened
to look my way

it says, like, I want you
to know I think your head-
phones are, y'know,
a totally awesome
shade of black

After We Deplane

someone has the job
when the pilot drops
the ponderous bird back
to earth, when passengers
and bags pour out
of its portals like eggs
from a spider or maggots
from an open wound

someone has the job
when the flight crew
thanks us, smiling
in so many friendly
languages for riding
over clouds and mounds
of brown and green below

someone has the job
when we come to roost
when the great bird nests
before it rises once again

someone has the job
of cleaning out the cisterns
that pend beneath the lavs
where we go to piss or shit
or vomit or just to stretch
our legs a little when
the seatbelt sign is off

and of course someone
knows the better job is up
in business class or first
someone knows to work
up through the ranks
to where the pool is clean
and clear and odorless

unlike the fetid mess
left behind in economy
by the rest of us

Ten Minutes Before Boarding (Gate C7)

she sits alone among her close friends
Gucci, Fendi, and Prada
her coat a down-filled Burberry
hides her rosebud mouth behind
hair glistening like a black
satin cat

he leans, professorial, smug
over her shoulder from behind
cradling a Starbuck's venti

she cringes in her faux-fur collar
as if he whispered sadistic fantasies
she could never quite forgive
or his mouth
stunk of last night's prawns in garlic
or this morning's bitter coffee
black, no sugar

her mouth a jagged gash
in the offence of her paling face

he leans in again, on the attack
she parries with the screen
of her iPhone, its cover dusty rose

his Razr Maxx responds
with a face the green of April rain

thumbs stutter on the glowing glass
a fever of furtive conversation

now she does not balk
as much, her shoulders fall a little
the rosebud starts to bloom

he leans in once more, softer

she does not pull away

About the Author:

James K. Zimmerman is a four-time Pushcart Prize nominee and award-winning poet – most recently the Edwin Markham Prize and the Pat Schneider Award. His work appears or is forthcoming in Miramar, Pleiades, Chautauqua, American Life in Poetry, Nimrod, The Evansville Review, and Kestrel, among others. He is the author of "Little Miracles" (Passager, 2015) and "Family Cookout"(Comstock, 2016), winner of the 2015 Jessie Bryce Niles Chapbook Prize.

SUNRISE KID
by Ross Jackson

On a windy day

from the footbridge look down
at city pavement
Chinese musician plays his erhu*
as a pigeon lays dots round

a half circle of idlers' feet
two African men are tall swaying masts
see that straw hat removed
by unforgiving gusts

what little depends upon
that yellow plastic bag jerking like a drunk
down the gutter of the street?
remind me imagist poet*

*Erhu- a Chinese three stringed fiddle.
*Respect due for the late William Carlos Williams.

Sunrise kid

his line of sight between smooth cream
vee of sugar gum's double trunk
whiskers sprout radii of gold
from puckered areola of sun
pulls on his pistol, fires one out
a messy shot which dries off slow
under fast climbing light

Humanless places

These places seen from the train are never
destinations

Dulled toothaches from a chalky past
the rotted abattoir on a coastal swerve
the once was jetty under the cliff
On weekends, empty Chem Labs
with lights still on, that remote bit
of hospital where a chimney
pours black smoke
Creepy, how they make you feel?

But especially
electricity farms screened by castor oil plants
fenced with steel bars:
colossal cabinets with coiled wire hairdos
steel/rubber chess pieces eight metres high
ceramic stacks
Fritz Lang meccano
naval mines and whisky stills bolted
on to concrete acres

 (Post modernist sculptors, take note
These are sub stations. Eat your hearts out!)

             Imagine tending these monsters
in darkness

Dawn comes up a burgundy sunflower
This is the real deal
This is lethal power

Dazzled by smartphones

before breakfast
swiping away
beside the forest pool

sunrays glance tiny panels
of leaded glass
on a dragonfly's wings

yellow waterlily hearts
open to beaded bodywork
of the drone

bobbing lily pads
touch and go spots
for each sortie flown

such delicate touches
touch and go spots
on the smartphone

About the Author:

Ross Jackson lives in Perth. He has had work in many Australian literary journals and some of his poems have appeared in New Zealand, Ireland, England and Canada. He writes about the experience of aloneness in the suburbs, about aging, visual art and other topics.

AS MEN

by Talon Florig

As Men

As men we are taught that a woman's walls are to be conquered, their gates to be crashed. We learn that only in the thrill of the hunt will we find the sweetest kill. We are taught that aggression is the surest path of a companion. Modern man pursues because "not interested" just means "hard to get." I've learned that a hunt is the surest path to a corpse because she keeps trying to killing herself. I think that we pursue prizes not people. I discovered aggression leads to hatred. I've learned crashing gates and conquering walls makes me a siege weapon and I've never known a battering ram to be a compassionate lover.

Night Life

My body doesn't let me
Drink with my friend
I'll take
Ginger ale
Instead
Of a fiery whiskey burning down my throat to
the cheers of my companion.
I'll take a water
At 11pm

Homeless Baggage

When you live from couch to couch the only luggage you bring is the knowledge that you're not good enough to stay

When someone lets you in the only question that follows you through the door is: when are they going to ask you to leave.

So you cart your burden on your back or bike but it always gets to their place first. It takes up the comfiest part of the couch so no matter which way you lay you're reminded that you cannot stay

Friends might house you for a night or 2, but then you migrate from coffee shops in the morning to bars at night hoping to meet someone new because: "John will let me crash Tuesday and Friday, but what the hell am I going to do Wednesday?"

But each time you sleep on their furniture or floor you've used up a piece of the universe's good will. So you try to give it back. You look for proof that you aren't just a sinkhole person pulling whatever scraps of charity you can. You cook breakfast, buy them coffee with your last three dollars, and pretend to be a conversationalist. But in the back of your mind you are just wondering if they have a spare mattress.

When you're homeless in your 20's you end up with a homeless heart.

Sure, best friends, strangers and everything in between can give you a warm place to sleep. But you will never let yourself stay.

Hiding. Losing.

Hiding things is never a skill I developed
Losing them, now that's something I've been practicing.

Atomic Metaphors

I didn't mean to leave my metaphors here
Sometimes they just spill out of my skull and end up on the floor
And try as I might to scoop them up before someone hits their head from slipping on my words
I do miss a few
They sneak away from my clean up crew
arms and rebound all around the room
Like Little Landmines left lying around.
We all have nuclear arsenal hearts
I'm sorry I didn't keep mine under better watch and lock
I keep giving the access codes to anyone who strolls through the fucking door
And even though I bolted my bunker shut, and layered it in concrete
my walls still crumble crack
And these atomic metaphors slip through the seams
Each Heartbeat. Detonate.
I hope you can forgive my missile operator negligence.
These hand grenades loaded with shrapnel spiked words
Were never meant for you

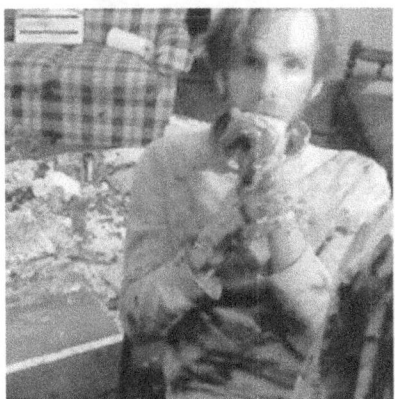

About the Author:

Talon Florig is a slam fist heart break panic attack put on paper. His metaphors are blunt instruments used to beat the past into submission. Talon writes about shame, regret, pain and suffering, sure. But Talon always manages to instill a sense of hope in his words.

A DUAL PERSPECTIVE
by Patrick Erickson

Black-eyed Susan

A sometimes upright annual
with alternating basal leaves
and stout branching stems
covered by course hair

hence brown Betty

It has daisy-like flowers
with yellow ray-florets
compassing brown or black
dome-shaped disc-florets

thus yellow ox-eye daisy

The genus name Rudbeckia
honors Olaus Rudbeck

a botany professor
at the University of Uppsala

and one of Linnaeus's teachers

Look for the flowerheads
in late summer and early autumn

Look for them in Maryland
where they are designated the state flower

Look for a blanket of them
in the winner's circle
around the winner's neck
at the Preakness Stakes

The roots of the black-eyed Susan
are an astringent

a wash for sores
a poultice for snake bites

an infusion for colds
and worms in children

a diuretic
and eardrops for earaches

Butterflies are drawn to them
in large color-masses.

A DUAL PERSPECTIVE

Does the edge of glory
really work?

Are you skittish?

Are you skirting
the edge

walking the walk
toeing the line?

Does it glow
like the glowworm

like its double
its wormhole
its twin

like those lighting strips
that direct you
down the aisle
to your seat

in a dark theater
full of dark matter
full of suspense
and no repose?

Are you sitting down
for this

or teetering on the brink
and over the edge
and down the wormhole

coming out
God knows where

the edge of glory
or the razor's edge?

If I could support
light waves

if I could refract light
like that

if I could be
on their wavelength
on the button
on the beam

I could put them on
I could wear them
as a gown
multi-faceted

if I could arc
like that

if I could refract light
like a prism

I could go the distance
I could be the go-between

We could all be
as one

and go for broke.

LIKE JOHN CAGE

I could say
"Take my heart"

But what of my heart strings?
Snap!

What of my rib cage?

I could say
"You can strum my ribs
if you can play me
like a fiddle"

like John Cage

no strings attached

Like John Cage
I could whisper
sweet nothings

But then the silence
would be deafening.

TWO STICKS IN THE MUD

Can two sticks in the mud

should you have two sticks
to rub together

compete with green reeds
much less commune

when the cattails
along the river bank
ever fluent
speak in tongues?

Can a tongue-tied couple
so entwined
enmesh

when one is root bound
and the other rootless

when mud meets mud
root upon root

the Sea of Reeds
one day

the River Styx the next?

About the Author:

Patrick Theron Erickson, a resident of Garland, Texas, a Tree City, just south of Duck Creek, is a retired parish pastor put out to pasture himself. His work has appeared in Grey Sparrow Journal, Cobalt Review, and Burningword Literary Journal, among other publications, and more recently in Adelaide Literary Magazine, The Main Street Rag, Tipton Poetry Journal, Right Hand Pointing, and Danse Macabre.

ANOTHER HOME POEM
by Daniel Ruefman

Another Home Poem

Are homes places to which we cling
longer than we should,
as if we are paint chips flaking
from the doorjambs,
or foam insulation bleeding
through the seams of splintered siding.

Or are they places we wish to grow
but perhaps shouldn't,
as though we were crab grass,
baked and brittle on the stone and dust
of a gravel drive, lacking the depth
needed for our roots to take hold?

Or are they just these guarded places
where we linger, inviting people by,
saying "come in, show me yours,
and I'll show you mine?"

Mine home is here, in this yard,
the one where impossibly muscled pitbulls
drag towing chains across deep ruts
carved in their crescent runs,
and my truest friends will stand at the gate,
and without opening it say
I see you and I understand,
careful never to come too close.

Arthur

There is little that I remember of my grandfather
but the fishing on Lake Erie.
Even now, I see his silhouette perched
atop an upturned five-gallon bucket
on the concrete pier at Presque Isle,
in the shadow of the small lighthouse there;

For bait, I think he preferred salmon eggs to worms,
as there was always a small jar in his tacklebox,
tiny ruby orbs suspended in brine,
so much like Lilliputian maraschino cherries,
that I once plucked one from the jar,
placed it on my tongue⬚ and I never did that again.

I think he must have worn a lot of hats
with the brim pulled low over his eyes,
perhaps to shade the light as he napped,
or maybe it was just to hide the whisper
of his chemo-thin hair, after he began
the too-late treatments for the Lymphoma
that metastasized, just as his retirement
was coming on;

Dad blames the postwar paint shop,
the toxic fumes he huffed
since his honorable discharge
from the Army Air Corps
where he trained soldiers stateside
to find Nazi targets for the B2 Bombers.

I can see his shape, skeletal thin,
his taut suspenders heaving up slack slacks,
his firm grip on the hilt of his rod
a patient patient, waiting for a fish
to rise.

I try to recall my grandfather's face then,
But it eludes me,
so I call up the sepia photograph
of the cocksure corporal hugging to him
a nurse with the eyes of my grandmother;
it is all I have of his face,
and I must be content with that.

Deserted City

The doors to LORD
are closed now;
the library,
where my aunt worked
was dismantled, shipped
south to another state,
its bones here reduced
to red-bricked rubble
tucked into piles
behind chain-link
and razor wire.

Across town
the mills rot in the sun
along the new Bayfront connection;
corroded sheet-metal eaves
crumble under their own weight
just visible over the stamped concrete walls,
waiting for gravity to bring them down

The oily stink of new blacktop
hangs off State Street
where rusted-out,
over-priced cars
replaced the Koehler Brewery,
two-blocks away
from the site
of another bankruptcy auction
at Lovell Manufacturing.

Just outside the city proper,
GE Transportation abandoned
the borough that it built,
back when barbers were doctors,
bleeding their patrons,
venting veins as it sought equilibrium,
hoping to remedy an imbalance in bodies
that never existed.

Tears of Johannesburg

Clouds grieve over Johannesburg.
Their underbellies slit
by the needle top of Hillbrow tower
until the streets surge.
In the alleys on higher ground,
good Samaritans pick their battles,
choosing which woman's screams to answer
and after how long.

In the pubs, voices chant
You can't save them all
while a government worker
speaks of the need for condoms
in a city where bruises bloom
on cheeks of wives
and sisters
and daughters
without any apparent cause
without any sign of ceasing.

In contrast, there are just 100 days
left in the dams in Cape Town,
where fields crack between rows of signs
from Monsanto, DuPont, Syngenta.
At least there is food from last season,
graywater to flush the toilets,
and hope enough for the woman
clinging an infant to herself,
staring up at dispersed contrails
seeing them as potential clouds

something that could bring
tears from Johannesburg
to fill the western rivers tomorrow.

About the Author:

Daniel Ruefman's short fiction and poetry has appeared widely in periodicals, including the Barely South Review, Burningword, Clapboard House, DIALOGIST, Gravel Magazine, Red Earth Review, Sheepshead Review, and Temenos, among others. He currently teaches writing at the University of Wisconsin Stout.

DEAR HERON

by Danielle Hanson

Dear Heron

You have grown tired of my presence.
I am a ghost haunting the wrong house.
You are the knowing inhabitant of my ineffectiveness.
I am what happens in the hour when clocks fall forward.
I am a lost hour of Spring,
In Fall, I am erased.
Have no regrets▯ migrate from my absence!
I will remain as a black rock rolling over in water,
as a ghost bound to earth,
as the weight of honey-soaked feathers,
as the stones eaten by birds to crush their feed.
You will remain the night, rising from the earth at dawn.

Things that disappear

A colony of sea snails as the lava hits water.
Laughter as you realize it's not a joke.
The memory of sweet during bitter.
Love, as she sees from across a party,
the look you give your wife.
Night in a spotlight.

After we capture the scenes on the camera,
we must destroy the camera to be free.

Small Dove

Small dove,
why do I not take pictures of you
as with your flashier brethren?
You walk near my bench bobbing
in agreement with the day.
And then walk away, hoping
you haven't been seen.
Stay –
I will not bother you
except perhaps to hold you in my hand,
to pet your soft back and coo at your smallness.

About the Author:

Danielle Hanson received her MFA from Arizona State University. She is author of Fraying Edge of Sky (Codhill Press Poetry Prize, 2018) and Ambushing Water (Brick Road Poetry Press, 2017). Her work has appeared in over 50 journals. She is Poetry Editor for Doubleback Books, and has edited Loose Change Magazine and Hayden's Ferry Review. Daniellejhanson.com.

SUNWASHED AND WASTED
by John Sweet

a beautiful failure

like dogs running
through frozen fields

like february sunlight on
dirty ice

blue skies cut by powerlines and
dying gods left where they lie

abandoned factories
and empty warehouses

this is the place

meaningless words casting
distorted shadows and you w/ a
full tank of gas

you w/ a loaded shotgun

the last 20 years of yr life
spent turning in the
wrong direction

choosing not to choose

closing yr eyes whenever
the crucial moment
came near

taskwatawa

pull you from the fire
drunk and you are blinded
and you are blind

a visionary wrapped in
gauze and feathers

a patient dog, like magritte,
and the revolution is
in your mind

the boat is sinking, but
we are surrounded by desert

we are buried beneath the
golden haze of sunset

the future screams down
toward us without mercy

the sky, blatantly

With your unused coupons,
with your losing lottery tickets,
not raped but beaten,
on the floor and bleeding,
a baby crying in another room,
a man with a question,
a cop,
asks how long ago it happened,
asks why no one here stepped forward
to save Christ,
and the room is a cell,
one of the walls is made of bars,
and you're naked,
tied to a cot,
and the stranger with the gun wants an
answer that you don't have.

Your arms have been broken.

Your tires have been slashed.

Man at the door says he loves you
just before he kicks it down.

sunwashed and wasted

in the corner office
looking out over the desert

in the blood of upstate
where men with no faces talk
about simpler times

you slaughter the buffalo
and the indians will die

you spread disease
with a generous hand

culture is a cancer of course
and what it feeds on
is other cultures

the children run away but
really
where else is there for them
to go?

forget place

focus on the
shock of realization

the horse with its head
thrown back and throat cut
wide open

the soldier with his eyes
burned into blindness
with his hands
mutilated beyond repair

will you laugh when you
tell him that the war
has been won?

season of invisible explosions

About the Author:

not a man but a house on fire in a
waterless land, and it's a
foregone conclusion growing old this way,
growing useless with your
raspy voice and your shaking,
bleeding hands

it's one thing to be loved and
another altogether to be wanted

your job is a prison

your family is hungry

seven days now with the
edges of your heart scraped raw
against the idea of suicide

cold sunlight, wind blowing through
open wounds, through the spaces
between burning factories, between
trembling wires

thought you could build a house
out of your father's failures,
out of anger,
and now you have a roof that leaks

no walls

no windows

a punchline without a joke and a
view of the cemetery, but
this isn't your town and these
aren't your ghosts

the phone never rings

makes nothing but a beautiful
sort of silence that you
can really wrap your mind around

John Sweet, b 1968, still numbered among the living. A believer in writing as catharsis. Avoids zealots and social media whenever possible. His latest collections include APPROXIMATE WILDERNESS (2016 Flutter Press) and BASTARD FAITH (2017 Scars Publications). All pertinent facts about his life are buried somewhere in his writing.

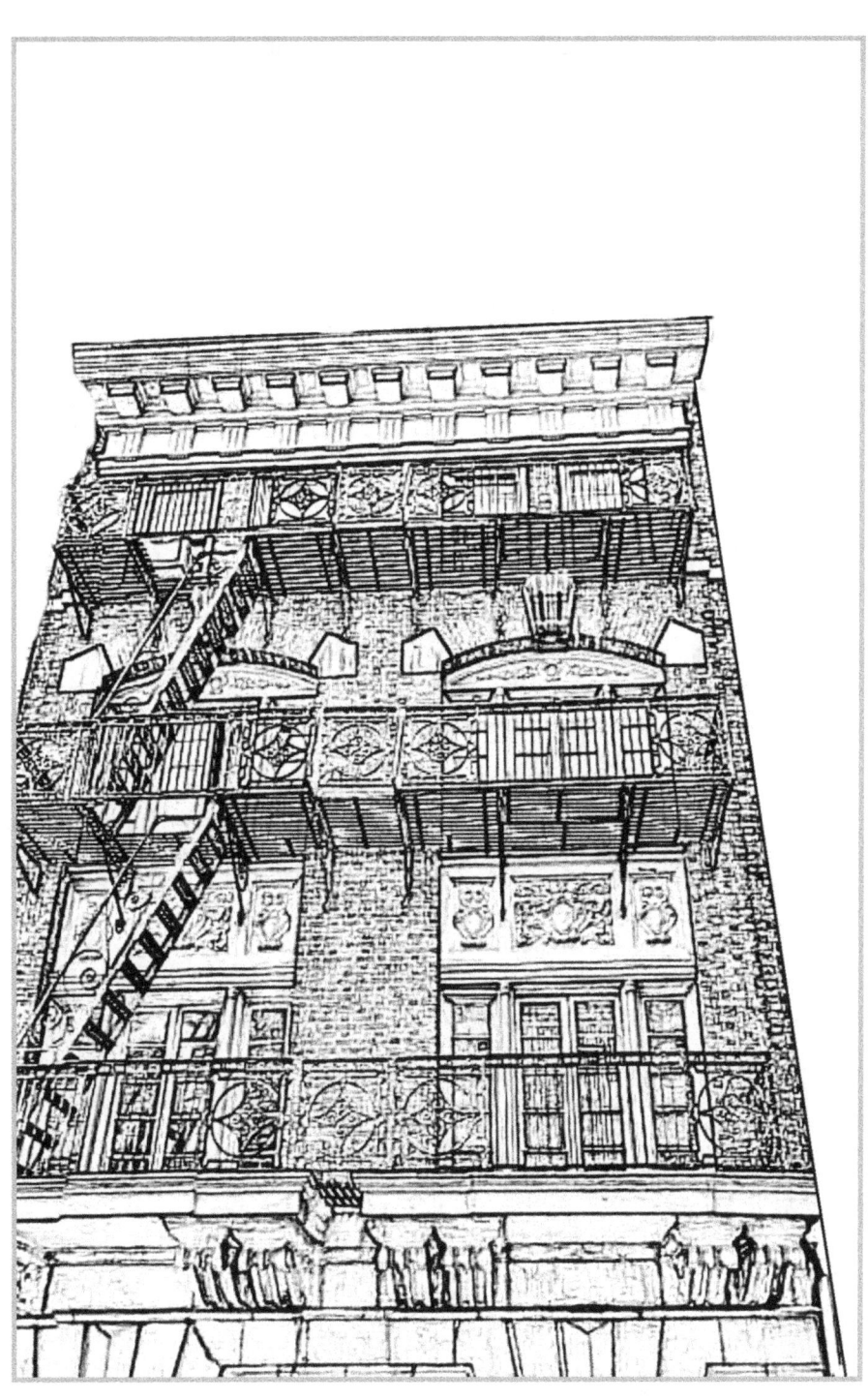

AT HALF-PAST TEN
by Souzi Gharib

At Half-Past Ten

At half-past ten
Our lane entombs the remains
Of the lingering rays
Of its homebound inmates
Under a lid of impenetrable hazel.

The moon has been banished for years
From sauntering down our cobbled pavements,
Some think we've been accursed ever since
That morbid murder in the cathedral.

I look beyond the canopy of boughs
And try to imagine clusters of stars
Decking my sable flowers with crowns.

My sullen kitten begins to mew
She's never been blessed with a lunar view,
Never licked a starlit drop of dew
That mischievously slid into its bowl of stew.

I peer through glass at sheets of black,
No house is distinguishable by a glow or spark,
No lamps splutter, no candles flicker out
In this half-past-ten, undiluted dark.

I retreat into the hall, descend a flight of stairs
To where my ancestors fermented their grapes,
Light seven rows of star-shaped votives,
Seven rows of crescents and full-moons
Then start investigating stellar nooks.

J.F.K.

In Massachusetts, Brookline, an ailing child
Was born to an ancient Irish clan,
A lineage of kings, heroes and bards.

For History and English he had a flair
But he had a date with world affairs,
A Call, or call it what you may.

Jack wooed billows, sails, and ships
The sail-boat Victura was the birthday gift
Of which many doodles were scribbled on scripts.

Palm Beach, Cape Cod
Rhode Island, Newport
Would bear testimony to competitive sports,
Swimming and sailing, the family cult.

A naval career was a natural course
To command the PT-109
Out of whose wreckage he salvaged a friend
Then carved deliverance into a coconut shell.

The Senator, the Congressman
The youngest elected President
With 'Date Nolite Rogare' had hailed each task
The ancestral motto: 'Give, be unwilling to ask'.

The White House became a menagerie
Of a wide range of endearing pets,
The animal-loving Kennedys
Doted on their constant friends:
Leprechaun, a pony from Connemara,
Shanon, Clipper, Strelka, Pushinka...

His name remains resonant
With navigators and saints
With St Brendan, St Columba,
And Jeanne d'Arc on a steed,
With St. Francis, with anchors,
With steering wheels,
With bottlenose dolphins,
With fleur-de-lis,
And the golden fleece.

Heritage

I had imbibed from you a passion for rhymes
For Le Rouge et Le Noir, for Arabian Nights,
In your own footsteps I became a girl scout,
Our rowing boat was a replica of yours,
And swimming is a communion with a fellow being
Whose blood has the same amount of salt.

I have a date with history
I've written a treatise in defense of Templar Knights,
I pursue traces of King Arthur
In Glastonbury and Wales,
And Camelot is a fortress
Which is built in the heart of faith,
My inevitable journey to Avalon
Will eventually unite me with your grace.

I listen to your favourite song
That of September, my favourite month,
D. H. Lawrence was born on its eleventh
And tree-leaves have a date with the wind.

My room is either too hot or too cold,
And when it grows too icy
With no heating whatsoever at home
I listen to Richard Burton's Camelot
To feel your warmth.

With your youngest brother Bobbie
I share an unremitting pursuit
Of evasive justice,
Of a sense of righteousness,
And like the affectionate father of eleven children,
I remember my graces at meals
And every night before I sleep.

We both take after St. Francis
Who befriended the natural world
We have fraternized with mammals
With fish, with birds, with stone.

The Homecoming

You broke away from your bodyguards
To join a choir of boys
Who sang "The Boys of Wexford"
To welcome you in your ancestral home
At Dunganstown.

You laid a wreath at the John Barry Memorial
The father of the American Navy,
The name resonates with heroic anchors
But with music simultaneously
With the music theme of The Persuaders,
Of Somewhere in Time, my favourite film,
Of Dances with Wolves,
Of Mary, Queen of Scots,
Of A View to a Kill, James Bond's.

At Arbour Hill in Dublin
You paid tribute to the martyrs of 1916,
In Limerick you quoted an old song
An invocation that kindles a come-back to Erin
Éire go brách

Ireland may not be your country of birth
But it is held with the greatest affection
You are bound to come back with shamrocks
With Springtime, a lover's return.

1963

Charismatic Jack had a rendezvous with death
Was shot by the malicious bullet in the head,
The membrane held precious by Druidic Celts,
On Friday, November, the twenty-second.

The dark-winged agent
Had aimed at his brain
But the un-armoured name
Remains un-slain
A fort,
A Camelot,
A peace refrain,
A concept which no bullets can amputate.

About the Author:

Susie Gharib is a graduate of the University of Strathclyde (Glasgow, Scotland) with a Ph.D. Her doctoral thesis, entitled Stylistic and Thematic Reassessment of The Trespasser, is a critical study of the work of D.H. Lawrence. Since 1996, she has been lecturing in Syria. She self-published four collections of poetry (My Love in Red, The Alpine Glow, Resonate and Kareem) and a collection of short stories (Bare Blades). She is a lover of Nature and enjoys swimming.

THE INCESSANT PRAYER
by Olga Kawecka

How the Gothic world laughs by its joking gargoyles
At this epoch of nothing! And the azure is bright,
Like the hundred and thirty-third psalm, over mires;
And the distance is clear after the violent fight.
All will be immortal in the Kingdom of the

Almighty.

All is but a contour of the perpetual day.
Many are called... And the hallow fire is lighted
Under the sorrowful vaults, to illumine the way.

2017

All will be just for the better.
Do not listen to the world,
Whose speech is but a clatter
From the hollows of Naught.

2017

The Incessant Prayer

Father, help the one who is crying;
Help a heart which is waiting in vain;
Help a poor one who is dying;
Help all those who are in pain.
Oh Father, I pray for all losses,
For all those who languish with grief.
Thus a restless wave surges and groans
Neath an overwhelming dark cliff.
Listen to my inexpressible prayer,
Which is throbbing, like blood, within me!
May all sorrow, anguish, and care
Change to happiness, and may peace be!

2017

In memoriam ***

I am unable to retreat.
I taught myself to go forward –
through the dark,
across the unknown,
in spite of pain.
When I could not go
I crawled.
I never looked back,
at the void.
I learnt to fight circumstances
and my body.
Now I have to struggle with the pain of loneliness
tearing my soul into flames of despair.
And I shall fight,
for your sake;
I shall do what I must.
Maybe, my battle will be lost,
but I cannot retreat.
I am going forward
to spite the torments of the human void.
For your sake...

2017

Author about herself:

I am a poet, prose writer, translator, and historian; author of fourteen books.
I was born in Tver (Russia) in 1987, but my ancestors came from Poland.
Literature enthralled me since my childhood. I began to write poems at twelve (a desperate longing for true friendship was their main idea). At the age of sixteen, I published my writings for the first time.

In 2007 I went to Tver State University (the Department of History). The same year I set to an intense self-education, which lasted six years. It included history of Europe, Russian and foreign literature, biographies of poets, European art, history and theory of classical music, the First World War (mainly the Western Front), and other subjects. I learned nine languages (including Latin and Aramaic).

In 2013 I published my first book. It was a collection of poems and poetical translations from nine languages into Russian. Then there followed other books: three collections of poems, a collection of photographs taken by me at an old Polish cemetery in Grodno (Belarus), a novel about the Swedish composer Joseph Martin Kraus (1756-1792), etc.

I am greatly obliged to my friend Artyom Kouznetsov, who inspired me to live and write.

L'ARUME
DA LLISBOA
por Jose Manuel SÁNCHEZ

<table>
<tr><td>

TIMES SQUARE

Times Square.
Marzu, 2017.
La Hestoria convidome
a chumar un treitu.
La Hestoria,
-díxome ella-
fai tiempu que punxo'l so llar
en Nueva York.
Ye un bon llugar
-díxome ella-,
pa decatase
de que de xemes en cuandu
ye posible
algamar los suaños

</td><td>

TIMES SQUARE

Times Square.
Mars, 2017.
History invited me
to have a drink.
History
-she told me-
was living for some time
in New York.
It is a good place
-she told me-
to understand
that sometimes,
it is posible
to reach the dreams.

</td></tr>
</table>

L'ARUME DE LLISBOA

Ye'l peor llugar del mundiu
pa escaecer a les muses,
pa escecer al amor braeru.
Ye ellí au ñació la saudade.
Ye un llugar
p'entamar a escribir poemes,
anque nun seyas poeta.
Ye un llugar
qu'arreciende a océanu,
a llonxanes aventures,
a viaxe (el mio arume preferíu).
Ye un llugar
au tolos nómades s'afayen.
Falo de Llisboa.
Tuvi na ciudá fai venti años,
pero alcuérdome más del arume
de la ciudá
que del arume
de munches persones
d'aquella dómina.

THE LISBON FLAVOR

It is the worst place in the world
to forget the muses,
to forget the true love.
It is there
where the saudade was born.
It is a place
to begin to write poems,
even if you are not a poet.
It is a place
which smells like the ocean,
like the distant adventures,
like the travel
-my preferred flavor-.
It is a place
where all the nomads
feel good.
I speak about Lisbon.
I visited the city
twenty years ago ,
but I remember more
the flavor of the city
than the flavor of a lot of people
of that period.

XUEVES	THURSDAY

Nun sé si dalguna vegada	I don't know if sometimes
chumasti daqué	you have drink something
nel Lake Street Bar.	in the Lake Street Bar
Ye un chigre allugáu'n Brooklyn.	It is a bar located in Brooklyn.
Yo taba de pasu	I was visitng
-yo ero un eternu nómada-	-I am an eternal nomad-
na capital del mundiu.	the capital of the world.
Ellí pescancié lo que ye	I understood there
un oasis lloñe de casa.	what is an oasis
Una nueche,	far from home.
un xueves,	One night,
el pinchadiscos punxo	one Thursday,
un canciu de Los Ramones.	the Dj put a song
Paecía un xueves	interpreted by The Ramones.
na mio propia casa.	It seemed a Thursday
	in my own home.

About the Author:

José Manuel Sánchez was born in 1970 in Grau (Asturies, Spain). He holds a Ph.D. in History (University of Oviedo) and he is anthropologist. He also studied Tourism and has earned three Masters (History, Protocol and the third in Philately and Numismatic). He published several books in Asturian language and papers and articles in various journals and reviews.

SHANGHAI (2015)

Prestame la nueche
de Shanghai.
Son les tres de la mañana.
Abaxu, al delláu del hotel,
atopo un chamizu abiertu.
Merco una cerveza Tsingtao.
Préstame tar equí, lloñe
de tolo que fui,
lloñe de tolo qu'ero.
Ye una nueche d'eses
qu'enxamás escaezcen
los que ñacieren
pa ser nómades.

SHANGHAI (2015)

I like the Shanghai's night.
It is three in the morning.
Below, near to the hotel,
I find a store open.
I buy a Tsingtao beer.
I like to be here,
far from all I was,
far from all I am.
It is one of those nights
which never will be forgotten
by all those who were born
to be nomads.

HORRU DE TIEMPU

Esti poema foi escritu
al atapecer
pa escaecer
que barafustié
una xornada más,
pa escaecer
que caltengo
nel mio horru de tiempu
una xornada menos.

Esti poema
ye tolo que fexo'l mundiu
güei por min,
ye tolo que fici yo
güei pol mundiu.

TIME GRANARY

This poem was written
at nightfall
to forget that I have wasted
one day more,
to forget that I preserve
in my time granary
a day less.

That poem is all
what the world have done
today for me,
it is all what I have done
for the world.

A SONNET TO MY HUSBAND
by Cassidy Manley

A Cancer Poem

He died on a September day
But you could say
He died all year
Or forty six
It rises from his skin like mist
And dew-like, settles on
The couch
We threw away
But the smell remains.

It's hard to clean a living room
When the problem is invisible

But I sit and it pools
Around my hips
Until I am damp with the stench of

Death
Has an odor best described
In water words -
It churns and seeps
Into your clothes
Your skin, your nose
Drip with
The fetid breath
That left his body

Clung to my hair until I could have wrung it out.

A Sonnet to My Husband
(or "Why Did You Throw Your Phone at
the Airport?")

Were you born with a yell perched on your lip
And ruler's iron spoon clenched in your teeth
I do not know the rocks where you were reared
I tide-like raised submissive to the beach

I cannot grasp the low-slung power hung
Between your thighs save when I grasp to take
Your edicts into my unwilling hands
Which cannot know the fists your fingers make

Was your father an earthquake in your home
Of tremor shaken mothers that began
With woman after woman long perplexed
By the deep seated anger of a man

And I born of the sea to stay your hand
To know and know you not, borne to the land

About the Author:

C. Manley is an actor, student, and New Hampshire native. She currently lives in Dayton, OH with her husband and their impish corgi. This is her first published piece.

NAVEL

by Edward Lee

NAVEL

Every time,
without fail,
before they make love,
she picks fluff from his navel;
there is always fluff there,
even straight after a shower.

It is their ritual,
her finger in his navel,
before lips lock,
hands roam,
and he enters her.

They barely speak of it,
it is just the done thing,
a cleansing of the body
before the emptying
of desire.

But, last night,
and two nights before,
with her lips tight against his,
her fingers remained her own,
even as he entered her;

they fluttered above her head,
far from any part of him,
dancing almost,
or signing thoughts
of her distraction
as she waits impatiently
to explore the navel
of some new other,

someone now worthy
of her thorough cleansing.

MOURNING

The trees outside my window
are weeping leaves,
not in sympathy
to the pain in my heart
at your sharp sudden absence,
but simply because
autumn has fallen.

LIVING FOREVER IN THE NIGHT

In my garden
I speak to the night,
throw my voice
into the moonless dark,
not looking for,
or expecting a reply,
simply wishing to add
something of myself
to the endless darkness,
my words turning
to winter, clouding
in the air,

and disappearing, disappearing,
the night taking it all
as its own,

and I turn
and reenter my home,
my skin prickling
as it moves from cold
to warm.

BORN

Heartbeat born
of my heartbeat, but
I will always be
a stranger to you,
another man your father,
your mother my lover
when she shouldn't have been,

and yet
should have;
heart plus heart equaling
the possibility of forever.

Should I speak,
raise my voice
for your ear,
and in doing so
rearrange your life,
when maybe your life now
needs no rearranging,
a change in its course
nothing but cruel interference?

I have no answer
that doesn't spark further questions,
and maybe
that is an answer
in itself,
an answer for now,

now.

EMPTY EYES

The endless darkness
of the cow's eye
saddens me
as we slowly drive through
the herd, while
potholes and bumps
shake my stomach
to the edge of sickness.

Through the window
I can hear the cows
moo, moan,
as they continue on
to wherever the farmer
is taking them,
abattoir or milking plant,
and we, free of the herd,
speed on to where we are going,
a place I can't remember,
my mind lost to the eye
of the cow,
the abyss of its soul
sucking all I knew
down into itself,
my sense of self,
my identity
not even a whisper
in my mind;

even as the car stops,
my father announcing,
"We're here",
before he and my mother
get out of the car
and enter wherever here is,
my sickly stomach
is the only prove
I have
that not all of me
disappeared into deadened bovine
eyes,
while moo-ed moans
echo faintly

About the Author:

Edward Lee's poetry, short stories, non-fiction and photography have been published in magazines in Ireland, England and America, including The Stinging Fly, Skylight 47, Acumen and Smiths Knoll. His debut poetry collection "Playing Poohsticks On Ha'Penny Bridge" was published in 2010. He is currently working towards a second collection.

His blog can be found at
https://peanutsfromthecheapseats.blogspot.ie

and his Facebook page can be found at
https://m.facebook.com/edwardleewriter/?ref=bookmarks

OPEN UP

by Roger Singer

OPEN UP

There was an unwillingness
of movement.
A stretch like tree tops
in a tempest.
A few indistinguishable words
slipped clumsily into the air.
The visions were intangible;
the ones
you think you touch but
fail to feel.
It was a spirit dream, a
celebration of aesthetics.

A temporary creation of
interior thoughts like
running through water;
a beating of the heart in the
seconds between where one
survives.

Radiant neon heaven lights
strike a course across the eyes,
stirring them open
to a morning world.

CREATION

I settled down,
though briefly and had
a think,
like when water becomes
ambient, not warm or cold;
placid while reshaping an
outcome.

It was a must, a brush with
orderliness, creating the back
end before leading the pen
to water.

It became a flower moment,
an opening as if sun touched,
bringing up the curtain,
reducing the haze of disturbance,
holding the thoughts back
so the first word could lead
to verse and then story.

About the Author:

Dr. Roger Singer has been in private practice for 38 years in upstate New York. He has four children, Abigail, Caleb, Andrew and Philip and five grandchildren. Dr. Singer has served on multiple committees for the American Chiropractic Association, lecturing at colleges in the United States, Canada and Australia, and has authored over fifty articles for his profession and served as a medical technician during the Vietnam era. Dr. . Singer has had over 890 poems published on the internet, magazines and in books and is a Pushcart Award Nominee. Some of the magazines that have accepted his poems for publication are: Westward Quarterly, Jerry Jazz, SP Quill, Avocet, Underground Voices, Outlaw Poetry, Literary Fever, Dance of my Hands, Language & Culture, The Stray Branch, Tipton Poetry Journal and Indigo Rising.

EACH CORNER

There was a glass reflection
of sky and overhanging branches
as we passaged down river,
slipping through calm water;
an excursion through nature's lyrics.
Each wide corner revealed another
portrait in perfect color;
small gatherings of birds swept
silently above.
There was a balance. A quiet
tempest of greatness. An
undercurrent of power not seen.
A language of deep motion with
ancient voices.
The potential unlimited.

LUST

by Stephanie Daich

LUST

Is there an emotion more powerful than you?
You have found the way to rule the world.
Once you have slivered your way into a human heart
You take over all logic and reason.

You know how to control a human mind,
Pushing out sanity, causing the mind to go mad,
Forcing thoughts of obsession on foolishness;
You become the controlling emotion.

Oh lust, Hollywood markets you in the billions,
Clothing lines exhort you, and ad agencies love you.
Money is tossed your way without resistance.
You play with the feelings and spread lies.

Empires crumble because of your influence,
Kingdoms walked away from, possessed by your lure.
Because of you, families are destroyed and
Educated people make fools of themselves.

Oh lust, one can hardly escape your influence
In this world. The soul has been sold in your name.
You counterfeit love and ravish sensibility.
Is there no way to stop your disease?

Where's Daddy

"Where's daddy," his daughter cries through the night.
"Where's daddy," his precious cries at first light.
He had been there so often to tuck her in
And always there with his morning grin.

Her face lost some of the sparkle it had
Because she doesn't know what happened to dad
She looks for him in the faces she see
But none of them are who she needs them to be.

They buried him in the ground last May
She thought the funeral was a party to play.
She doesn't understand where her best friend went
While family is sad and often lament.

"Where's daddy," his princess cries each day.
"Where's daddy, why did he go away?"

Offended

While surrendering his will to another,
While his own happiness he does smother,
While filling his soul with hate,
Once in, it's hard to escape,
He ties his own knots, and binds his own chains
All happiness gone, only bitter remains.
And although the slight by another, unintended;
The "victim' chooses to remain offended.

Who Am I

Deep inside
my own life
I do hide

I want to
show who
I am to you

But you don't
want to see
you just won't

The person
The real me
who's within

Who am I

This is what they expect of me
Propaganda everywhere.
This is who they want to see
When at me they stare.

Pre-described social ques
Belonging to their sect.
Limited, closed off views
That I'm supposed to perfect.

What if there's another way
A different path to trod?
They think my path does stray
When something new I prod.

Maybe how they choose to view
Isn't always right.
And even though it might be new
They burry it out of sight.

Who am I supposed to be
When the person inside I must oppress?
And never show the real me
The me, I must repress.

About the Author:

Stephanie Daich is a correctional nurse who has diverse opportunities in the insight of human experience. As she sees a vast array of emotions, she explores and reflects this privilege in some of her writing. Often, herwork focuses on self-change and empowerment. Some of the realms Stephanie has been published in are Angles to Bear You Up by Judy C. Olson, Angles Watching Over You by Judy C Olson, and Making Connections: Interdisciplinary Approaches to Cultural Diversity.

MY PANTRY

by Rikki Santer

Still Life with Whoopie Cushion

It ain't lowly novelty for Madame who likes her money
straight up with all faces facing her, she the supreme curator
of cheap laff exotica. Behold her credenza draped in lustrous
black velvet, read her realm from left to right fixed
in one silenced moment of thigh-slapping theater. Fake fly
sprawled atop a Mortimer Snerd incisor, overbite
sublime; alabaster bust of Soupy Sales, rivulets of dried pie
cream at his neck round his bulging eyes. Sinews of Renaissance
light frame this hearth of tactical jokes that hold us in their spell.
Not a porcelain platter of purple figs dripping with juices,
but a crude heap of smashed trick fingers with assorted breaks
in their rubber skins just ripe for alarming; fat pitcher sweating
its cherry Kool-Aid grin with a dribble glass tipped
in mid-weep; whoopee cushion all ego all vanity, pink pearly,
viscuous flesh promising razzberry succulence. This still life frames
the language of monkeyshine. Not broken bread, vacant oyster shells,
or lemon rinds spiralling but the spillings of Cachoo powder, fabric snakes
spent and sprung from peanut brittle cans, and a dappling of puddles
glistening plastic puke or doggie doo. Through the room's beveled
window, clouds hover wearing our voyeur moustaches,
tips twirling upwards Snidely Whiplash style.

Secret Nights on Loop

Rising from the brittle fur
and oily scales of sleep,
I swell on each ledge of night
wedged between two bulbous
knees of defeat. Acrobatic
thoughts chafe: will
I lose my balance
on this too taut
trampoline?
Never a simple
now but a how
will next words
unwrap the cardboard
face of next day?

I am open rust,
yellowed light
mourning over stars,
permanent-press tumbled
too long in the dryer.
Each night I awake
to this dark room,
bed in a web
of black yarn, strands criss
cross me into tight-fisted
memory, singed premonition,
a maniac hill of beans.
I ache for a holy equation
to release me yeast-like
through the two-way mirror
promising gently baked
golden brown day.

Betty Boop Marries Herself

Her camel kneels
& Betty steps down
into the midnight Ganges
feels the gentle push
of the current
when she submerges
the pearl halo of
her linen robe tiptoes
into the swirls
and eddies
of the river's open
throat. Her voice
lightly bebops
the waters to sleep.
She feels the barge
of napping monkeys
make safe passage
from her vagina
dentata. Calla lily
behind her ear
she launches
into the darkness
a leaf bowl
filled with
frangipanis,
her carved love
spoon a confident
oar. Betty's curves
dissolve into the tender
pull of current, red
petals bobbing
to the surface
like a menstrual
milky way.

Arboreal

When the March storm wouldn't spare punches
and our front yard elm snapped in half,
its broken body collapsed across the driveway.
The luxuriant crown sprawled across the wet black,
rasped for lost sustenance. Impotent,
I watched from the window and notched
my life with yet another tree:

The billowing pink bouffants of dogwoods
that intoxicated my young daddy,
the weeping willows that forgave
my parents' fights--

My brother and I crawling under skirts
of a cul-de-sac's giant pine, our secret
club for beheaded Barbies
and stolen cigarettes--

First kiss along the river
in the sticky hollow
of a trunk's furry bosom,
my mother's glow as confidant--

The sheltering pin oak that won
my father's heart when he made
his first downpayment
for an abiding couple's grave--

Sentinel twin maples that celebrated
my homecoming from every morning run,
three witness oaks murdered by our
next-door neighbor, grieving crows for days.

Each spring, tree men troll to our front door and swagger
their chainsaws for internment of our broken elm.
But we adore our stubby Pippi Longstocking
in ballerina's fifth position, buoyant
branches sprouting for the sun.

My Pantry

Crowded with shelves it knows how to shelve
canisters of worry that pretend to be hermetic

and brave. Good at orderly conduct
but bad at assortment and prayer. When

you gingerly open its louver doors
baby moths will sprinkle the air.

My pantry nourishes latent messages
and stir-fries hope that's gone stale.

It oils a gluttony of delicacies yet
garnishes with flavors too frail.

I don't fear indigestion. or lament what's
gone pale, but I question this pantry's

duty to what should be kept in the dark
versus what to yoke and impale.

About the Author:

Rikki Santer's work has appeared in various publications including Ms. Magazine, Poetry East, Margie, Slab, Crab Orchard Review, RHINO, Grimm, Slipstream, Midwest Review and The Main Street Rag. His fifth poetry collection, Make Me That Happy, was published recently by NightBallet Press.

Adelaide Literary Magazine

OUR FIRST THREE YEARS

adelaidemagazine.org